Ryan Weston has been both a lifelong student of history and a diesel mechanic for his entire adult life. This conflicting duality has not been lost on him, either. In his pursuits with the former, he has been a reenactor, living historian, paid public speaker, world traveler, and has earned a degree with a focus on history. He now brings these passions together along with the grit of his daily life as he adds the title of author to this extensive list. He lives with his wife and cats near Chicago, Illinois.

To my wife, Sarah, without whose tireless support this book would not be possible.

Ryan Weston

# P IS FOR PICKELHAUBE

AUSTIN MACAULEY PUBLISHERS™

LONDON • CAMBRIDGE • NEW YORK • SHARJAH

**Ordering Information**
Quantity sales: Special discounts are available on quantity purchases by corporations, associations, and others. For details, contact the publisher at the address below.

**Publisher's Cataloging-in-Publication data**
Weston, Ryan
P is for Pickelhaube

ISBN 9781685627843 (Paperback)
ISBN 9781685627867 (ePub e-book)
ISBN 9781685627850 (Audiobook)

Library of Congress Control Number: 2023912948

www.austinmacauley.com/us

First Published 2023
Austin Macauley Publishers LLC
40 Wall Street, 33rd Floor, Suite 3302
New York, NY 10005
USA

mail-usa@austinmacauley.com
+1 (646) 5125767

I owe a great debt of gratitude to all the friends and family who supported me in my adult educational journey, this book is an unexpected and happy product of that struggle. To that end, I would like to thank my professors at Moraine Valley who recognized my latent talent for writing and who encouraged it, especially Professors Hogan and McIntyre, the latter spurring me on with the now prophetic "dude, you can write!" I owe an endless debt as well to Frank and Stephanie Wegloski, who besides from offering family support, have directly provided both technical assistance and their considerable artistic talents towards the creation of this book. I would also like to thank Tyler Anderson for not only being an incredible barber, but also a creative sounding board for innumerable ideas, some of which have found their way into my writings over the years. And finally, I would like to thank James Hetfield of Metallica for writing and recording the song 'One'. That singular work both lyrically and visually is responsible for starting in my youth what became a lifelong obsession with the Great War, and which in turn lead directly to the writing of this book. Art begets art, let it inspire you.

# Table of Contents

# Author's Note

This novel was written from the perspective of both German and French combatants of the First World War. As such, to the best of my ability the language and vocabulary used reflects that which would have been appropriate for this conflict and era. Definitions for all military terminology can be found in the proceeding glossary, and all instances of the French or German language being directly used in the text have been translated in the glossary as well.

*Post Script*: For ease of operation and for the sake of uniformity, despite this conflict having many names it is universally referred to as the 'First World War' throughout the glossary of terms.

# Foreword

The First World War, or 'Great War', was a war fought in many theatres by a diverse host of nationalities from 1914 until 1918. It is mostly remembered today for its elements: Trenches and poison gas, submarines, the Lusitania, and 'poor little Belgium'. But it is as often as not overlooked today due, in no small part, to its much larger and more destructive successor, the aptly named Second World War, which occurred scarcely more than 20 years later. Yet numbers and statistics do not tell the entire story: What the Great War may have 'lacked' in scope and numbers, it more than made up for in brutality, futility, and horror, while paradoxically accomplishing little militarily. The Great War systematically dehumanized its participants with an overwhelming onslaught of new technologies in what would later come to be known as the first instance of 'Industrial Warfare'. Individual soldiers were rendered meaningless as were their individual exploits in battles that lasted for months and that featured casualty counts that often mounted into the millions. In just four short years, centuries of European military traditions were forever obsoleted by the unspeakable carnage on the battlefields and destruction in urban centers, and what emerged afterwards was nothing short of an entirely new version of Western Culture.

R. E. Weston, July 2018

# Chapter One

How do you process death? Is it easy for you? Or was it? Like anything I suppose it gets easier with repetition. As in, repetition of incidences, not multitude of. Experiencing a multitude of deaths at once is a difficult thing to do unless you're in a line of work where that is a common occurrence. And even in that case, it's only not difficult because of the commonality. It can still be difficult otherwise. In any case. How was your first time? Was it everything you pictured it would be? Did your first time make you feel good? Was it someone you knew or was it a complete stranger? Did you care for them? Was it quick and painless? I suppose like everything else your first time is never what you pictured it would be. It probably happened before you were ready, too. And probably with the wrong person. We always picture our first time being with someone really special and memorable. Which I suppose is a silly thing because of course your first is always memorable, your first of anything is memorable. But were you ashamed afterwards? Angry you hadn't hesitated, or been more patient? Or more ready? But who's ever ready. You think you're ready, you might even have that someone in mind. But then it just happens. And then it's over. Then you've had your first time and there's no going back.

My name is Kurt, I'm Bavarian by birth, and I don't like talking about my first time experiencing death. Or about sex. Or about my first time experiencing sex. Sometimes I get embarrassed when someone asks me about my first time and I get fidgety and end up mixing up my first times in my head. I get all mixed up and then don't want to talk about it and just want to go somewhere and not be talked to. But sometimes, you have to talk about it. Sometimes the person who asks you to talk about it is a person you can't say no to.

There are a lot of people in the world you can't say no to. Especially if you're a little boy. Little boys by rights don't really have many people they can say no to, except perhaps other little boys. Little boys think that they can say no all the time but they don't realize that their no doesn't really mean no to too many people. The same is true of being in the army. When you're in the army you can't say no to really anyone except maybe other soldiers who are just like you. You can't say no to anyone else who is higher up than you, but they can say no to you. So being in the army is like being a little boy; you either stay little and therefore cannot say no to anyone, or you get bigger and then can say no to the boys who are smaller than you.

My name is Kurt, always has been. Even when I was a little boy. Even when I was a little boy who lived in a little house with his little family. Lived with his little family in a little house next to a great big forest. A forest big enough to hide in. Big enough to swallow you whole. My name was Kurt even then, even when I was lost in the woods.

Lost is a funny word. So is found. Lost doesn't always mean something is gone, it just means that you can't have it anymore. Found doesn't always mean that something is back. It could mean that someone else has lost something and that you now have found it, making it yours and not his. Sometimes what you find is not at all what you lost, but it becomes its replacement and you soon learn to forget what you lost in the first place.

When soldiers go missing from the roll call, they are called losses. Losses whether they are dead or alive. Either way, they are lost.

# Chapter Two
# Les Allemands

"I can still remember the first one I really saw up close. That was a completely different world then I suppose which is almost a strange thing to say. Or maybe at any rate, it was a world inhabited by a completely different sort of people. We were all different, proud, special people then, who had names and goals and ideas and mothers and fathers that were proud of us. Nothing like us here today, standing in this raped and God-forsaken wasteland. Everyone was so proud and happy to be off on an adventure, to be a part of something meaningful and grand. All so eager. Too eager. I know I was eager, and eager to add to my father's already impressive record from the War of 1870. We all knew that this would be a repeat of that short and glorious little war and that was one of the reasons why we were all so anxious to be off and to be a part of it. Yes, yes, it was different then." Through the glare of the evening's Very Light display, I could make out that Unteroffizer Pangloss' eyes were misty, and barring the emotion of his wistful tale I assumed that his NCO ration of schnapps might have been the culprit. "It was nothing like I really expected. We were on the move, long columns of men with nothing to look at but the backside of the soldier in front of you, when we came upon and skirted the remnants of a small village that had been laid waste by heavy artillery, probably our own. Minus a few hollow and burned-out houses, everything was either flattened or churned into a crater, and everywhere was a fine white stone dust that made the ground crunch under our hobnailed boots like a layer of hoarfrost in a grassy meadow. Our line of advance had brought us down into a small dell, which once crested brought us face to face with him: He was off to the side of the road splayed out over a water ditch. It was the better portion of a French peasant, his lower portion having been shorn away grotesquely as had most of his face. His lifeblood had long since drained away and all that remained were his blackened insides trailing away from him like some hideous sea creature. All down the line the men in front of me were jeering and whistling at him, or even kicking pebbles off the road at him as they passed. But as I drew nearer, I discovered that rather than feeling boastful or jovial that I was instead mesmerized and found that I had a difficult time looking away as we marched past him. This, while at the same time secretly inside, I was glad to have seen a dead Frenchman since this somehow in my mind gained me access to some exclusive little club. Little did I know then how open membership to that little club would be, for all of us. Somehow the image of that dismembered little man and his red shirt and brown jacket has never really left me despite all I've seen since. There have even been times that I swear that I have seen him lying on a battlefield, or crumpled in the bottom of a trench, or submerged in a flooded shell hole…" Pangloss took a long drink from his tin cup that I hadn't noticed in the darkness, confirming my suspicions. "Like a big red mushroom grown in a dark bog. No, like a bright fall leaf floating in a dun-colored pond. That's what he looked like. A splash of color in that otherwise white landscape, and just the tramp of our boots and the jangle of our equipment as we marched past…" His voice trailed off as he turned his head and peered out into the night. Unteroffizer Pangloss was an old-timer to us, an original. One of the Kaiser's old hands. He had already been in active service when the Austrian was shot, and he was one of the many eager young men who with the help of our grand strategy was going to be in Paris within a week of commencing. We all were a little awestruck by his presence and of course talked up his legend to the endless stream of replacements that came and went through our lines nearly continuously.

Yet, the question always remained in the back of our minds, "Why only an Unteroffizer?" We'd all seen the brass spikes sew stripes on men for the most trivial of accomplishments, and have known many a Sergeant who was no different than the men he was supposed to lead and ended up dying along with them just the same. Yet Pangloss was a pretty good soldier, and in many of our humble opinions should have progressed up the food chain by now. "No, he was like, like an oil painting that the artist accidentally swiped with a brush that had the wrong color on it. A bright color that was completely mismatched for the scene that he was painting." Okay, so he carried on a bit when he drank, but his nights were haunted even worse than ours were. Just by sheer arithmetic he had seen more death, had killed more, and had lived amongst the dead

16

longer than any of us in our small section. So we cut him some slack when he rambled. Plus when he got drunk he tended to share his schnapps and cigarettes with us *frontschwein*.

# Chapter Three
# Die Franzosen

I hate it. I hate having it. I hated wearing the awkward and noisy thing and question why I ever insisted on buying it. When I have it on I am constantly aware of it, and must be mindful not to submerge it or knock it too hard on something as I go about my daily tasks. When I sleep, or try to sleep, I try to hide it under something so that the incessant ticking can be muffled and I can be less reminded of the passage of time. Then too, there have been times that I have woken up just to wind it, fearful as I am of it stopping running in the middle of the night. My wristlet, my badge of rank to the men as much as the stripes on my greasy uniform jacket, is a tool and a piece of equipment reserved for only those who made the rank of NCO or higher. It sent men to their deaths, along with my whistle. Tonight I have it resting on a bench wrapped in an old handkerchief, with my pistol belt and gun laid over it. They sent men to their deaths too, and none of the above discriminated. I guess it was working, the handkerchief that is, because I was starting to focus on the moaning of a *poilu* that was coming from somewhere in the trench near my dugout. I suppose he was dreaming, though none of us really slept deeply enough to dream unless we went to bed rather under the influence. I for one have never gotten over the feeling of vermin crawling all over me as I lay down to rest, nor have I gotten used to the muffled noise of rats consuming the war's detritus within the surrounding earth of my hovel. The moaning has stopped. Now I hear my wristlet again. I am starting to flip through my mental inventory of things that I can wrap it in to quiet the God-awful ticking when suddenly a sharp explosion tears through the night from somewhere out in the trench before my dugout. I leap up from my cot to my feet, sending the rats scurrying and my blankets flying. Before I can move, a second blast shakes me to my senses and confirms my earlier suspicions. Grenades! We're under attack! All is confusion. I dash to my bench, throw my wrapped wristlet onto my cot and my pistol belt over my shoulder, and manage to grab my closest companion as I dash out toward the door—only to be greeted by a roar and a flash of light. With a sharp percussive rap, a grenade explodes just around the corner, the heat and debris rush past my face as the explosion briefly lights up the scene of confusion and horror around me. My ears are ringing. All is chaos. Do something. Suddenly a cry from the darkness. "Sergent Clouthier, what should we do?" Instantly, I am in focus. I scream into the dugouts that I know flank mine.

"Out! Out! To arms! We are being raided!" Within seconds worried faces emerge from the darkness with shovels, bayonets, clubs, and *le vengeurs* in their hands. Another grenade erupts off somewhere to my left, followed closely by more screams.

"On me! Follow me!" I draw my pistol and push forward toward the melee ahead. As I approach the next cut in the trench the telltale whistle of a potato masher sings over my head.

"Get down!" I cry just as it explodes off and to the left of my little band. Another scream. I rush around the corner and see a *boches* about to pull the cord on another grenade. In an instant, I raised my pistol and let loose its feeble payload—and am reminded for the umpteenth time that for some reason this pistol always hits lower than it should. I know I aimed for his head but I seemed to hit him in the leg, given how he hobbled off after I hit him. Just then I'm pushed to the side as my brave band rushes past me. They could sense the timing was right and they were correct, the *boches* attack has bogged down in confusion. All the typical sounds follow: Screams, gurgles, coughs, thuds, tears, clangs and bangs. Shovels cleave neck bones, clubs bludgeon heads, knives pierce chests and faces, pistols bark out with their sharp reports. Men drown face down in the muck of the trench as others stand on them to get a better footing for the next opponent. I see my wounded friend from before. He has tucked himself into a corner and is waiting for his moment to either flee or draw blood once more. My hand runs down the side of my pistol belt and feels for the clasp that unleashes my fearsome companion: My nail. Despite the haphazard issue of *coutrots* and *vengeurs,* I have never wanted to replace it. It has been with me since the beginning, and has probably killed more men than my ridiculously inaccurate pistol has. Just as I was about to crouch down in preparation for the pounce one of my brave poilus shoves me aside and rushes toward him. He's been spotted! A brief exchange of blows ensues, but tonight

France has the upper hand. The *boches* is face down now, and my man is kneeling over him, repeatedly driving his knife into the back of his skull. I put away my nail and switch back to the pistol, but the show is over here. Only sporadic pops and groans and a few brave rifle shots come from the trench around us, and I know those are just the wounded being dispatched and the survivors being chased off. In any case, it won't be long before the customary flare and machine-gun show starts. For me, it is time to gather up who is left and assess the damage here, which will be followed inevitably by a verbal report to the roosters on up the food chain. Looks like it will be another sleepless night for me, though at least there might be brandy at HQ.

# Chapter Four
# Les Allemands

Lars was looking glum this morning, and rubbing his elbow nervously while wincing a little and shifting from foot to foot. Nobody was really saying much, a few men were smoking and everyone was thinking about the rations that were supposed to be on their way up. "So I heard that things didn't go so well last night, huh? What was the matter? Did you piss yourself when you saw those scary little boys in blue and their pointy little kitchen knives?" Jürgen was an asshole. He was a natural bully, too: Big, broad shouldered, and easily 15 centimeters taller than the rest of us, he was always giving everyone a hard time. He was very proud of the large tattoo that he had over his chest too, and was constantly walking around with his tunic off and shirt open so that everyone could see it and see how strong he was. I'm sure it got him inside a lot of barmaids before the war but few of us really gave a shit about it here. "Shut up, Jürgen. We didn't take you along because we needed men who could think for themselves and keep their mouths shut."

Lars was not particularly fond of Jürgen and enjoyed giving it right back to him. Plus he undoubtedly risked his life last night on the raid (though we had yet to hear about it) and so was feeling naturally a bit punchy this morning. "Oh? Well then tell us, brave defender of the Fatherland, what *did* happen last night to cause the deaths of most of your squad at the hands of those little Frenchmen?"

"Well, Jürgen, had you ever been chosen for a raid you might know a bit of what you are talking about. On a raid, everyone has a job. I was picked to be a bomber. As a bomber you are given an old sandbag with a rope through it that is full of hand grenades and you have your club or shovel at your side. As a bomber, my job was to bomb." At this, Lars rubbed his elbow again. I tried to look and see if he had blood on his coat there but I couldn't tell, we were always all so filthy. "There were 12 of us, led by a Sergeant that I didn't recognize. Another bomber and myself, and then 9 men plus the Sergeant for the killing and capturing duties." We were always trying to capture someone on our night raids, I guess the Junkers in the officer corps were convinced that we would be able to glean fantastic information from this man once we had dragged him back to our trench. We all knew better: Even if we *did* manage to bring someone across no-man's land alive he would undoubtedly know about as much of the French battle plans as we did of the German—which is to say next to nothing. "So we crept out last night, sliding along on our bellies through the openings the pioneers had made in our wire, and almost immediately I managed put my hand right into the rotting chest of a poilu which caused me to practically vomit. I probably would have, too, if I wasn't so worried about the rats that I had stirred up when I found that rotting piece of France's own. Anyhow. When we got to their wire, the two men with cutters got to work while the rest of us all laid really still and alternated between listening for sounds and watching for flares, and of course, checking that we didn't lose anything as we crawled over. This gave me a minute to look the Sergeant over: He looked scared, and kept opening and closing the flap on his pistol holster nervously which I didn't like. When the wire was cut us bombers slipped through first, followed by the rest. At a word, we both spread out and then took a leap of faith into their trench." Lars didn't know it, but he was starting to sweat. I could see the beads forming on his forehead. And he was rubbing his elbow almost constantly now. I also noticed the greenish black slime that was all over his side which made me realize that he wasn't making up the bit about putting his hand in a poilu's corpse. To Jürgen's credit, he was listening like a schoolboy, and hadn't said anything nasty since Lars' story started which was no small accomplishment for him, either. "I couldn't believe there weren't any sentries in sight! I took a grenade out of my sandbag and carefully unscrewed the end cap. When the Sergeant gave the word, I pulled the string and threw it—and then all hell broke loose. The other bomber and I were throwing down the opposite directions of the trench, and we must've gotten off almost a dozen between us before they began emerging from their holes. Now comingled between the explosions were screams and shouts: Pistols went off and a round embedded in the trench wall right next to me—close enough to spatter me with mud in the process—but I just got down lower and continued lob my bombs. It seemed to be working too since no one had made it around the corner from where I was tossing blind." I was starting to sweat now which is kind of funny. I mean, I wouldn't be scared to fight last night if I was there, and I wouldn't be scared of a fight today if it happened. I've been in combat plenty. But when I think about a fight, think about hurting a man, killing a man, I feel a little funny. I get uncomfortable—it actually makes me want to run away and hide. Killing makes me want to hide, thinking about it does anyway, but of course, I can't. I'm standing right here with nowhere to hide and I'm surrounded by my comrades, so I won't try to hide. Besides, Lars is a good story teller. "I glanced over my right shoulder and saw to my horror that our men were fully mixed up with the French in close combat. The other bomber had stopped! He must've been killed, which meant that their men were surely streaming down that side of the trench in droves. I looked for the Sergeant. I tossed another grenade. I took a few steps back and looked again, this time trying to see if I was the last man standing. Just then the piercing twang of a bullet striking metal pierced my ears as it ricocheted off of a steel sniper plate right above my head. Where the *hell* is the Sergeant? I knew it had to be time to go, and so I swung my now almost empty sandbag over my shoulder and grabbed my club from my belt." Ah clubs. Clubs. We all had such fantastic clubs, and I must admit that I've become rather obsessed with them lately. We all had gotten into the habit of carrying them on our belts, even when we weren't assigned to a raid. They made very effective tools for dealing with the rats, and besides, the sight of us all standing around with studded clubs on our belts made us feel like medieval knights, which somehow conjured up a distant sense of chivalry. I liked to look around at the different designs we all carried and wonder at their varying effectiveness. For instance, I have always felt that the designs with the exaggerated spikes protruding out of them would prove cumbersome in a melee, as the spikes might become embedded in an adversary or bent if they struck something hard, like a helmet. Locally, there was a machine shop set up behind our lines somewhere that made them for us, they were literally delivered up to us by the barrel. Everyone had one. The ones they made here were usually made with a rounded wooden handle that had an iron rod protruding from it. At the end of the rod was a cast iron head, usually a square or diamond in shape. I always thought mine was special because the head was five-sided, though at the same time, I've always felt it a little long for my liking. In any case, I liked it better than the ones I've seen with a spring and a weighted head on the end. I had asked a farrier who happened to have a bit and brace in his tool tray to bore a hole through the handle a few centimeters up from the end for me once so that I could thread a bit of rope through it, which gave me a better grip when swinging it. See, I wrap the rope around my hand if I can, which makes my grip very tight and lets me focus on my swing rather than just hanging on to the club. But regardless, no matter what the design they were such effective killing tools under the right circumstances—even within the tightest of spaces they developed considerable energy through a swing due to their weighted heads. I completely caved in a Frenchman's skull right through his helmet once with mine. Right through his helmet. Which honestly was pretty horrible when I think about it, which I often do. Again, it's funny— I love my club and I love thinking about my club, but when I think about using my club I start to get tense and start to feel like I want to run away and hide. This is the kind of shit that keeps me up at night sometimes, the sound that Frenchman made when I crushed his head with my club and then I didn't even wash it. Anyway, as Lars was saying… "Just as I grabbed my club a bleeding comrade grabbed me and yelled that we needed to go, *now*. As I was about to ask where the Sergeant was he was brutally stabbed in the back and fell down to his knees before me. Looking up I saw a wild-eyed Frenchman holding a knife and in an instant I caved in the left side of his face with my club. I then swung a leg up and jumped out of the trench and in the process saw a few figures running in the darkness toward our line. As I ducked through the cut in their wire, I snagged my elbow, and when I rolled on my side to free it a rifle round buzzed by me so close that it made my ears pop. I panicked and dropped my sandbag as I tore myself free, and just in time. Just as I got close to our line the flares went up on both sides, and then I'm sure you all heard the brave machine gunners let about a half a million rounds fly to re-mark their territories." At this, Lars turned and walked a few paces away. I went over to him because I assumed that he was upset. No, he was taking a piss. He always had such comic timing.

"You know, Kurt, if you came over here to comfort me like this, you're going to need bigger breasts." Lars smirked at me like he was winking at a girl in a beer hall, all the while still exposed from relieving himself. I laughed and went to shove him but as usual he deftly parried my blow, with the result that I almost pitched over onto the floor of the trench and into his piss puddle. He had such cat-like reflexes, which is one of the reasons why he was always picked for night raids—and likely one of the reasons why he kept coming back from them. Lars was my best and really only friend in the unit and had been ever since we met during our training—only to be assigned to the same unit by chance after we were newly minted as soldiers. We were nearly inseparable, and as such had experienced a great deal of this war together—both the mundane and the surreal. Through it all, through all the violence and fear, we'd developed a love and a sense of humor that had carried us though the worst of it. It would be impossible to explain to anyone I knew before the war the true goings on here, and even harder to expose loved ones to that macabre sense of humor that we've developed between the two of us. For instance, like the time we were filling sandbags from the soil of a caved-in dugout after a particularly heavy French bombardment, and someone in the pioneer detail struck a long-rotting corpse that had been unearthed with his shovel. Due to his exhaustion and work stupor, he shoveled the rotting pieces into the bag that his partner was holding like so much building material. We all snapped out of it when the smell hit us, and especially once we saw that both of them were covered in maggots. As everyone expressed his personal version of revulsion at the sight the only one to speak something intelligible was Lars, who simply said, "And I used to *love* spätzle so much before the war, too."

That was my Lars. "So, what juicy details did you leave out from your heroic tale of last night's raid?" I could tell that he had been holding back when he was orating earlier. "Kurt, I'll tell you this," and at that, he straightened up and looked around. "That raid wasn't child's play. The days of us walking over and strolling around in their trenches may very well be over. Last night was different, they fought like, *lions.*" And at 'lions' his eyes grew a little wider, which told me that he was being dead serious. "They somehow swept through our entire squad before I was even aware that things had fallen apart. Whoever that ass of a Sergeant was certainly paid dearly when they met him, I never even saw his body when I made my escape. For all I know, they hacked him to pieces right there on the fire step."

"What do you think happened? Do you think they rotated a different type of unit in our front?" Lars looked down and kicked a stone with a flick of his heavy boot. "I don't know, Kurt, from what I could tell they were just normal French infantry. No alpine soldiers, no Moroccans, no Algerians. They just overwhelmed us and that's a fact."

As Lars and I turned to head back over by everyone else who was milling around we heard a familiar voice. It was Unteroffizer Pangloss, who seemed to have attached himself to the detail of soldiers bringing up our breakfast. As we all instinctively fell into line with our battered eating utensils in our filthy hands, Unteroffizer Pangloss organized the detail into a serving line. "Alright men, no shoving. I do not need to remind you that this is to be shared by the lot of you." He always took on such an official tone when he was playing the role of his rank in front of a group. "I will dole out the coffee to ensure fairness." Great. He must not have ever noticed that no one was particularly greedy when it came to that commodity: It always tasted terribly, either because of what it was actually made out of instead of coffee beans or because the water used to make it often smelled like corpses. We shuffled down the line, making sure to only take our share. Black bread, hard sausage, a turnip, and coffee. As Unteroffizer Pangloss ladled my share of coffee into my cup I couldn't help but notice that it was both still hot and that it actually smelled like coffee. This immediately aroused my old-soldier suspicions. "Hey, Lars, what do you think is in store for us?"

"Why? Because the coffee is hot?"

We were almost always on the same page.

# Chapter Five
# Die Franzosen

"So I want to be absolutely sure that I have the facts of last night's incident correct in my head. A squad of German soldiers were able to cross between our lines, breach our wire, and gain entrance to our trench lines—all without detection? Is that correct, Sergent?" I was having a tough time focusing on what this Capitaine was saying to me. My ears were still a little sore from that German grenade that went off so close to my head last night. Furthermore, I was tired, and I couldn't tell what I wanted more: A cup of coffee or a short glass of brandy. In either case, I knew that I wouldn't be receiving anything if I didn't wake up and start to answer in a way that would earn me a drink.

"Sergent Cloutier, sir, I am Sergent Cloutier, and unfortunately what you have stated is correct. I cannot fathom at this time what possibly could have caused the egregious lapse in our defenses, nor can I account for the status of the watch sentries at the time of the attack, but I can assure you that my investigation will begin immediately upon my return." At this, the Capitaine motioned for me to sit down in the chair that was in front of his desk. His little dugout-office was typical of quarters this far from our main front line: It was still in a trench, and still muddy when it rained and plagued with lice and other insects, but it wasn't surrounded by or dug from ground that was impregnated with the debris of human beings like our little holes up toward the front were. He existed here in a world that while not safe from a heavy German artillery barrage if one ever came this far back, was all but removed from the otherworldly vista that I called home for the time being. "Sergent Cloutier, can I offer you a cup of coffee? My orderly has just brought up a hot demijohn." Looks like it was to be coffee and not brandy.

I'd learned from long service to never refuse either though so I accepted gladly. "Tell me, what is the status at the front? Are the men losing their fighting spirit? You must know that the type of thing that happened last night is not to be tolerated, and that we must maintain our edge without compromise." His coffee was much better than I had expected it would be, and wasn't full of the types of things that I had to typically skim off of the top of what I usually drank before I took a drink. "Without question, sir, our army and our men are as strong as ever. In fact, the assault, once detected, was repulsed almost immediately and resulted in an almost complete German loss. I can personally confirm even the death of the NCO leading them. If anything, sir, I will only say that long and uninterrupted service at the front has a way of numbing the senses, which is the only thing that I can account for the failure of the sentries. In any case, steps will be taken immediately to remedy this." At this, the Capitaine rose from his seat (to which I also immediately rose, almost spilling my coffee in the process). After saluting he bid me to leave, and in doing so, I made sure to finish my coffee and leave the cup on his desk where his orderly would see it and therefore tidy it up. Stepping out into the bayou that wound its way up toward the front I was instantly assaulted by the sunrise, which colored the dull and muddy world around me garishly. I lit a cigarette, and as I was heading back made sure to keep my eyes open for any opportunity that might arise. A good soldier never comes back from the rear areas empty-handed. Sure enough I passed a small group of soldiers unloading cases of Pinard at a crossroads in the trench system, and on account of my rank they didn't question me as I grabbed a few liters to take back up with me.

# Chapter Six
# Les Allemands

As Lars and I sat down to our morning meal and those around us did as well, the normal chatter began in earnest. Trench humor, trench gossip, and trench predictions: It seemed as if every facet of our lives now began with the word 'trench.' As usual the bread was mealy, and my turnip was soft, but the sausage was okay and besides, I've eaten much worse. "Boy, there are a lot of new faces coming and going around here these days. I cannot think that *that* many men have been lost to wastage and raids lately, and we haven't had a big stunt in forever." Lars took a bite out of his turnip and made a face. "Yeah, and I cannot help notice that Corporal Pangloss is not eating with us like usual either, but is instead back in the rear areas where he just came from with our food. I wonder if he went back because he forgot the strudel." At this, both Lars and I laughed, and then I quietly tried to remember what strudel tasted like in my head. Just then two strange faces plopped down on the fire step in front of us, plates in hand, and began to eat. They seemed to know one another but neither Lars nor I knew either of them.

"Hey, some food, huh? I can't tell if this is an onion or a turnip. It tastes like both. And I hate turnips. I could never stand them, and it used to make my mother so angry."

Neither Lars nor I responded to this new unidentified fresh face talking to us. He looked like a child. His uniform was clean, his face was clean and clean shaven, and furthermore, he was bright and peppy. Or in other words, he was a brand-new soldier. We both looked at each other and thought the same thing: they are reinforcing us here, something is up.

Just then Corporal Pangloss came around the corner (sans strudel, much to my dismay) and stood at the end of the section of trench as if to address us. The two new soldiers went to stand at attention but then realized that they were the only ones, and sat down quickly to the snickers of those around us. "Starting this afternoon, we will begin rotating work details from the front line into the rear areas for construction duties. The number of soldiers in this area have been increased overall to compensate for the movement of men and to maintain a defensive presence here at all times. Also, as some of you may know, last night there was a raid upon the French trenches opposite our lines. Unfortunately, despite the squad gaining access to the trench the raid ultimately was a failure. As a result, there will be another raid tonight, led by myself. I will make my dispositions as to the additional personnel needed after tonight's evening meal." We had all just been given so much more than bad food to digest. "So there it is, the answer to the hot coffee riddle. Something definitely is up."

"Yeah Kurt, I didn't like the sound of that—*construction duties*. What the hell could they be building that far away from the front line? And why do we need to help?"

As it turned out, our entire section was picked for 'construction duties' that afternoon. We were all marched back through the warren of trenches and out into the rear areas behind our line. This really was quite a long ways away from our front line, especially if you take into consideration how purposely complicated our system of communication and transport trenches were. We Germans were always proud of our ability to build things, and this subterranean world that we had created over these last two years was no exception. As we bumped along in the trenches, constantly squeezing past men in various forms of their various duties the murmur amongst us began in earnest. "So, Kurt, what do you think we'll be working on? I can't imagine that we'd be constructing a new trench line since it would be even further away from the French than the four that we already have are." Just then I scraped the edge of my helmet brim on the side of the trench, causing some small stones to rain down on the sides of it like hail on an awning.

"What?" Our coal-scuttle helmets were notorious for blocking sound, given that the wearer's ears are so far up into the design. This was both a bad thing and a good thing.

"Why don't you take that damn thing off and put on your feldmutze, Kurt! You're too far from the front line to have to worry about your head."

"You know I don't like taking off my helmet, Lars, only to sleep." Lars shot me a devious glance over his shoulder as soon as I finished what I had just said.

"And what about when you're with a woman? Do you take off your clothes and then put your helmet back on?"

At this, Lars started to laugh and almost instantly I did as well: Except it was almost nervous laughter for me. At the moment, I couldn't remember what being with a woman felt like and the more I tried to remember the more uncomfortable I felt thinking about it. Women in general made me nervous, made me want to leave. I mean, I had only been with a woman on three separate occasions, all of which made me feel really small when I thought about them and made me feel like I wanted to run away from everyone and to have some quiet time in the woods. Which is funny, I mean, I like women I guess, I mean… "Hey, what are we all doing? Where are we going? Should I have left my helmet back up front?" It was the new guy from breakfast who didn't like turnips. He was sweating along with his full pack on and looked like he had just arrived from a depot.

Since I was closest, and honestly because I was a bit friendlier with new people when compared to Lars, I replied to him, "What's your name, anyway? I'm Kurt, and this is Lars." Abruptly we came to a flooded portion of the communication trench, which temporarily paused our conversation as each man struggled to get through while keeping as dry as possible.

"Oh, I'm Rolf, and this is my friend Max." Max apparently was the other new fresh face from breakfast who had said nothing then and who said nothing now. I didn't realize before that he was rather portly, which made him stand out even more among us lean and hardened front line soldiers. He was panting quite pitifully, too, and was rather red in the face. I made a mental note of his feeble condition so that it wouldn't end up costing me in the future if and when a situation arose. Now through the mud, we could all talk freely again. "No, it was a good idea for you to bring your helmet. You may not need to wear it while we're working, whatever it is that that turns out to mean, but you'll be glad to have brought it if we come under some kind of fire on our way back up once we are through. I always wear mine, but you can switch to your feldmutze once we get to where we're going."

At this, Rolf's fat friend Max, who was trying his best to both listen to our conversation and to simply keep up, looked relieved. He apparently wasn't even going to wait until we got where we were going because he mid-stride pulled off his stalhelm and put on his crumple feldmutze, almost dropping both as he tried to swap one for the other. Lars, who was a few steps ahead and who I *know* was listening let out a short chortle, and then looked back at me and rolled his eyes.

Just then a halt was called. I hadn't noticed that we were now out on to the open ground behind our position, and there were many things to look upon in wonder at. For one, there were a couple of trees here and there, and a few green patches of grass, and I swore I heard a bird chirp though since I didn't see it I can't confirm it. All of the soldiers in front of me had their heads on swivels at this point too: It had been a while since our section had been rotated out of the front and I think everyone was feeling some sort of sensation akin to being reborn as we exited our anthill of a position. Once I was past the childhood wonderment however the rest of my new and temporary surroundings began to sink in. There were trucks moving clumsily on a dirt road that stretched off to the horizon, as well as horses pulling wagons and files of men marching. Dust hung in the air and there was cursing, shouting, and arguing as vehicles and men jockeyed for position on the road and all around were signs of something big in the works. Crates and boxes of every imaginable size were being stacked and sorted and the supply people were crawling all over them like flies on manure. We started to move again and as we did so I could see that we were being led off the road and toward a wall of trees that rose before us as we crested a rise. "Hey, Kurt. Have you seen Jürgen anywhere along the march? I don't remember seeing him, or having to endure any of his stupidity." At this, I then realized that I hadn't seen him either.

"I don't know, Lars, maybe he stayed up at the front, and maybe he was finally picked for a raid. Pangloss said that there was to be another raid tonight." At this, Lars threw his head back and clapped his hands loudly. "Right! Of course. Well, if we are lucky the French will be up and waiting for them, and perhaps then I won't have to listen to his shit anymore."

"Yeah maybe, but remember, Pangloss was supposed to be leading the raid. I wouldn't want anything to happen to him." At this, Lars didn't respond. We were all marching down into this little section of miraculously still-standing trees when we came to another clearing, this time surrounded by trees on all sides. Being the automatons that we are we immediately formed up as we saw an officer and his gaggle of orderlies and NCOs around him. Rolf went to say something next to me but I kicked him in the shin before he could get it out. I think he understood what I meant because he kept his mouth shut as the NCOs began to fan out from the officer, looking for an excuse to be brutal before one of their masters.

I kept my eyes on the officer standing next to his horse. He was every bit a Prussian Von which, being Bavarian, I naturally detested. His uniform was clean and perfectly gray, he had perfect knee-high riding boots on—complete with spurs, and the wappen and chinscales on his pickelhaube glinted brightly in the sun as he spoke to the group around him. As an added touch, he was even gesturing with a riding crop toward what I assumed would turn out to be our 'construction duties', though what really caught my eye was what was strapped to his waist. There, in perfect brown leather, was a large, boxy holster. It seemed to extend halfway down his leg and by the telltale taper of it could only contain one thing: A Mauser C96 machine pistol. *Wow.* I had only had the chance to see one up close once in my Army career, and that was way back in 14' when we were first mustered into the service. How big and exotic they were, especially with the shoulder stock attached. And they held so many rounds, too, and from what I understood they were considered to be the most powerful handgun in the world. I wondered to myself why this proud puffed-up Prussian—who probably hadn't fired a shot in anger since the *previous* war with France—would be carrying such a cannon. Probably for executions. Maybe the gun was so powerful that it would blow a man apart at close range, which really would make quite a statement to the witnesses. Or maybe, maybe it was to save ammunition. Maybe he could execute *two* soldiers at once by lining them up back-to-back and then shooting them through the chests. Unexpectedly I began to imagine the officer was looking at me, and while he did so he was slowly unbuttoning the flap on his holster like a man would the fly of his trousers before taking them off. I imagined he then reached into his holster and slowly slid the long, shiny pistol out like a man would his penis if he were aroused and about to put it inside, about to have, about to fuck someone. I could feel him watching me, I *knew* he was watching me, thinking about me, and I didn't like it. Much. I mean, not at all. I didn't like to be stared at by a man while he was holding his penis. I mean, his pistol. What was I saying? I meant pistol…I found that I had been concentrating on his pistol so keenly that I hadn't blinked for a minute and that my mouth felt funny and my vision was fuzzy. Squinting my eyes, everything began to come back into focus…the officer took a few steps closer to us, talking as he went while everyone followed behind him like a line of baby ducks. I could clearly make out a pink dueling scar that ran from his chin to his cheekbone on the left side of his face, as well as the Iron Cross 1st Class that was pinned to the breast of his field jacket. Due to how spotless it was I could even make out the Prussian 'FR' on the wappen of his pickelhaube which, had I allowed myself to do so would have caused me to chuckle since we Bavarians had many different ideas for what the 'FR' actually stood for. Anyway. I hadn't been this close to an officer of this high of rank since I left Germany and the sight was captivating regardless of my internal derision. Suddenly they all seemed to be in agreement: The officer walked over to his horse and mounted with the help of his orderly who then walked a few paces and mounted another smaller horse that I hadn't really paid any attention to. Everyone on the ground saluted and at that this Von trotted out of the woods and out of our lives. Lars cleared his throat. Portly Max shuffled his feet and yawned. Rolf sniffled. I adjusted my trousers and looked past the NCO that was stalking down our line menacingly for no real reason since no one was here to see him be tough. "Attention men! You will stack your non-essential personal belongings in the areas that have been designated. You will then be issued either a long-handled shovel or pick, and then assigned to a task and a work zone. The NCO designated to your zone will inform you of everything else you will need to know." At this, a few stout Sergeants moved out from the group and started giving orders to Unteroffizers. Before we knew it, we were being shuffled past a pile of backpacks, knapsacks, utility belts, and helmets that many a soldier was now deeply regretting having lugged along this whole way to now risk losing to the crowd. The lazy Unteroffizer assigned to 'watch over' the gear looked as if he couldn't wait to start rifling through our things once everyone was off and digging. Max looked longingly at his helmet when he set it down, and looked as if he was contemplating swapping headgear but he was rushed along by the crush of men before he could complete the decision.

Rolf turned to him as we were marching over to where we would get our construction tools. "Don't worry, Max, they had an NCO stationed just to watch over our things. Besides, you wrote your name in your helmet, right? Then there won't be any disputing whose it is once we get back for the day."

Lars and I shot each other knowing glances that basically said, "Welcome to the army," since we knew that if they had anything worth taking in their gear that they would probably never see it again. "You, shovel. You, shovel. You, pick. You, shovel." We were being issued our tools for the day. Lars and I both got heavy, long-handled shovels that would have been nice to have when we were digging our dugouts in the front line. Rolf got a shovel as well, but Max got a pick ax that looked like it would have been better suited on an Alpine holiday than the French field that we were standing in. At that, we were led to our work zone.

"You men have been given an important task. As you can see, the work has already begun on what will eventually be a grand structure. Your task today will be to dig where you are told to dig by your NCOs and the engineer officers that will be periodically stopping by for inspections. You have nothing more to worry about other than that. Carry on." Before I knew it, Lars, Rolf, and I were in a line of men, shoveling the heavy clay soil of France into wheelbarrows that were being carted off to a large heap some hundreds of meters away. Beyond that there were horse-drawn wagons coming and going that seemed to be carting away the soil that was being piled by us diggers. We could see Max with another group of men some distance off to our right breaking up ground that was apparently to be dug out as well. Where we were working was clearly to be the foundation of some great structure once we were done. The earth was dug straight down some ten or more meters and was cut smooth as if it was going to be a wall of some subterranean building. All around us we could see the outline of this huge structure taking shape here below the surface of this French field surrounded by a small forest of old-growth trees. The soil was very heavy and dense this far down as it was mostly clay, and with every effort the best I could muster was about half of a shovel full. "Goddamn, Kurt, what the hell do you think this all is? Do you think we are building a fort? Why the hell would we build a fort here instead of focusing on breaking through the French lines in front of us?"

Just as Lars finished that sentence an officer of the engineer corps walked past us behind the row of wheelbarrows. We hadn't noticed him due to the nature of our work and would have never spoken so freely in front of him had we done so. "You say that we should be worried about attacking the French?" In shock we all froze, shovels in our hand in various poses of the process of digging. "Why, but you are! Don't you know what you are building? It is called a Stollen, and it is to be used to house thousands of you *frontschwein* in safety while our heavy artillery pounds their positions to dust. After the guns are through, you will simply emerge and walk over the ground that their trenches once occupied and onto Paris!" At that, he walked off, hands clasped behind his back. We were dumbfounded. First off, an officer just spoke freely to us—which helped demonstrate the difference between an Engineer officer and a Regular Army officer but nevertheless it was still shocking—and two, he just divulged to us the apparent plans for breaking through the French lines and ending the war. Like I said, we were *dumbfounded.*

"Well isn't that something! Once we're all done here we will just put down our tools and walk all the way to Paris! We'll be on holiday! But does anyone know the way?" At that, Lars let out a giggle and then smacked me on the ass with the head of his shovel, to which several other soldiers around us saw this and murmured to themselves as they worked. I was about to retaliate when our ever-watchful Unteroffizer hove into view for one of his periodic observation walks. I straightened up and started digging again and pretty soon we were all back in rhythm as he stalked past. As I was digging the Engineer Officer's speech started to play back in my head. We were building some sort of temporary, yet stout defensive structure that would hold us in safety while our artillery pounded their position, which must mean that somewhere further away a grand artillery park is being assembled. I wonder how many of these Stollen there are. How many men will fit inside one once they are complete? A mixture of sensations began to run through me as I contemplated what this all meant. On the one hand, I was excited to be a part of something, and glad that there seemed to be a plan to break the status-quo that had existed on this front for the last two years now. On the other, my insides began to churn when I contemplated what it would be like to have to assault the French lines that were in front of our position, since surely they were strengthening them all the time the same as we were ours. Sure, their position was to be 'pounded to dust' by our artillery first, but what if it wasn't?

"Look!" My internal conversation was suddenly interrupted by our young friend Rolf. "Look up in the sky. Over there!" I rubbed the dust out of my eyes and squinted up into the sky, the brim of my Stalhelm shading my eyes like a visor. Lars stopped now too, and was using his hand to shield his eyes from the sun and searching all around him.

"I don't see anything. What are you playing at?" The tone in Lars' voice was about to turn sour when I first heard, then saw what Rolf was talking about.

"Shut up, Lars! Quiet!" Faintly, ever so faintly, could be made out a quiet droning in the sky. Way up in the clouds, thousands of meters above our heads, were what appeared to be a few aero-planes floating along. It was impossible to tell what kind of planes they were or whether they were German or French, or British for that matter. They seemed so small and far away, but after watching them a few minutes I could tell that they were staying over our position by flying back and forth. Rolf was very excited. "Are those our planes? I've never seen an aero-plane! Do you think they are going over to bomb the French?" Rolf's innocent comments did strike a chord: *Are* those our planes? And if they are, then what are they doing? And furthermore if they aren't, why isn't someone doing something about them? Just about now other soldiers began to notice as well, which created a general work stoppage in our area. This of course brought our ever-watchful NCO back over to encourage us to get back to work.

"What are you lazy fucks doing? Get your asses back to work, *now*! I can always recommend you all for a burial detail if you would rather dig graves!" The good Unteroffizer was right: Thank goodness his NCO training had included such extensive study in how to motivate comrades. All of us now feeling about ten centimeters shorter, we put our heads down and started digging again. But quietly. I think every man on that line was still listening for the drone of the aero-plane's engines. It was gone. No, wait, yes, yes it's gone. I quickly glanced up into the sky and looked where they were, but there was nothing in the sky now but clouds.

And then in an instant our idyll was shattered by the loudest and most terrifying roar I had ever heard in my life. The shattering noise was all around me! It was under me! It was in me! My head felt like it would burst! A roar like thunder! Chaos! Suddenly everything around us seemed to be either headed up into the air or falling back down from it. Trees! Carts! Dirt! Horses! Men! Pieces of men! Smoke and fire suddenly enveloped us as the world around us collapsed into absolute pandemonium. We were under a heavy bombardment! I dropped my shovel and threw my hands up over my ears as I fell to the earth, my mouth forced open by the sucking pressure of each successive wave. Explosion after explosion rent the air and shook the earth, to the point where my ringing ears could no longer discern one explosion from the next and I couldn't tell up from down. Suddenly a searing crash, a falling sensation, a ringing noise. Ringing. Ringing…I'm thrown to the ground can I get up yes I can get up I turn to yell for Lars but I'm not sure if anything comes out of my mouth boy my ears are ringing I stand back up Lars is running toward me with that silly stupid shovel still in his hands wait what a good idea I pick my shovel back up and then another *crash!* Off to our left the earth erupts like a volcano, sending wood, dirt, torsos and legs high up into the air. For a brief moment, I caught the sight of a stalhelm tumbling end over end as it fell from the sky and I briefly wondered whose name was written on the inside. In fact, for a moment I was mesmerized by it, and in a lucid moment imagined a smiling face still inside of it, watching this all happen without a care in the world. Then another fantastic *crash!* I'm shaken to my knees again damn my knee hurts Lars reaches me and collapses at my side he's been running and looks scared another thunderous Crash! I turn over to see Rolf standing motionless frozen in terror he should move his face is white his eyes are wide open his mouth is open he has soiled his trousers he should really move I spring up and dash over to him and as I grab him he snaps to… "Where is Max? Where is Max! Where is Maax!" I can barely hear him even though he is obviously screaming at the top of his lungs. In fact, I don't think my ears still work. Without a word I pull him back to where Lars is now furiously scraping out a hole in the side of the wall that we were just digging in front of. Just then it seemed as if the din was suddenly lifted like a heavy curtain from a window; I literally stared up into what seemed like the clear blue sky for a split second before my damaged ears picked up on a strange sigh, which was followed by a terrifying sound that I more felt than heard as an immense shell lands somewhere near to where we were digging, showering us with a great gout of men and earth as a portion of a smashed wheelbarrow lands with a thud uncomfortably close to the three of us. "Where is Maax!" Rolf is trying to dash out into the open ground again he really shouldn't do that we both see Max running our way through the smoke and flying debris he's not very fast oh look out here comes another *crash!* A shell lands off to our right and throws us to the ground and sends dust and clay everywhere my arm hurts I have dirt in my eyes Max is still coming somehow he's running full tilt shit that was close a shell lands near enough to drive splinters into us I have a few sticking out of my lower right leg I am grateful for this wall that we are up against Lars is doing such wonderful work scraping it out "Max!" Rolf is yelling to him but there is no way he hears. He is getting close now, maybe 20 meters away. "Max!"

A shell must have exploded in the air somewhere over where Max was running. I didn't really even hear it—all I was able to make out amongst the din was the queer sound of the cast iron case splintering in mid-air. Probably a time-fuse shell. Just as he was looking up to see us, his head was crushed and driven down into his chest with one stroke, the force of which was so great that it drove his torso down onto the ground and forced his broken legs to either side like a doll's. His body was literally smashed before us like an insect and tumbled into a broken pile by the huge piece of shrapnel that hit him. I instinctively spun around and started digging like mad next to Lars. He had made remarkable progress but his scrape kept getting filled in by the shaking of the earth and the flying clay over the lip of the now thoroughly ruined stollen foundation. We dug together frantically. My ears were completely numb by this point, or must have been, because I only felt the next explosion as it occurred somewhere around us…something hit me hit me on the back of my head good thing I have my helmet on oh I fell to my knees gosh do I have a hole in my helmet I feel blood running down the back of my shirt thump thump *crash!* How much longer will this go on why is it getting worse I stagger to my feet and grab Rolf who is staring at the heap of porridge that was once his friend Max he needs to move he goes limp when I grab him now I throw him into the scrape that Lars has made what a good scrape he has made okay now I can help Lars with the digging where is Lars oh there he is he's rising to his feet to get better leverage with his shovel when *crash!* A shell landed some distance behind us, but was still close enough for the energy to slam into us with incredible force. The shovel in Lars' hand was driven up to his face so hard that it threw him back against the wall of the stollen, rendering him unconscious. He collapsed onto the floor, blood streaming from his mouth and a nasty gash across his nose. I scrambled over to him and tried to roll him into the scrape that he had made and then to get into it somehow myself. I had just successfully gotten him face down into the scrape when suddenly my senses seemed to leave me…leave me…leave me…a crash! A flash…am I falling? Gone…it's gone…what's gone? Am I falling? I'm falling…*crash!* The ground…hard ground…my helmet is gone. My ears are bleeding. I am coughing blood. I try to rise to my feet but fall back to the ground. I try to scream but nothing comes out. I am alone. I'm starting to cry. I try screaming but I can't make myself loud. I feel like hiding. I am alone. I want to hide. I need to hide. I can't catch my breath. I need to hide. Where can I hide? I'm crying too much. I'm crying like a baby…

My mother had been in the kitchen all day, and the house was warm and full of the smells of her cooking in the most wonderful of ways. Everything smelled spiced and lovely, and my stomach had been growling practically since I woke up. My little sister and I kept creeping to the edge of the bannister on the landing and peering down at our mother, who was wearing her red and blue Christmas apron with the little gold bows sewn on it and buzzing around the house like a whirlwind. Father had been gone all day, but since it was Christmas Eve I had assumed that he was maybe at the market to pick up one last special item, or even at the toymaker's shop in town to buy one last gift for us. The suspense was killing me. I was so hungry, but my mother had made it clear that no one was to touch the food until father came home. I crept down the stairs and slinked over to where our Christmas tree was. My mother had already lit the candles on it and it looked so nice. I momentarily thought about snatching a candy off of it but I knew that somehow my mother would find out, and that an infraction like that could cost me my Christmas gifts or worse, send Krampus looking for me. Plus we knew that Saint Nicolas was watching…just then, the front door swung open with a crash. It was father! As he stood there in the open doorway snow came drifting in from the roof and fell gently to the floor in the hallway around him, sparkling as it caught the light on its way down. My mother came out of the kitchen to greet him but suddenly stopped halfway down the hall. Neither of them seemed to see me, and I felt myself shrink down next to the Christmas tree though at the moment I didn't know why. Father was what I was made to understand later to be beastly drunk, he must have been at the tavern in town this whole time instead of at home helping mother. He took off his hat and with difficulty his overcoat as well, but then slipped a little in the snow when he tried to remove his boots. He of course had his favorite little knife suspended from his belt, his *jagdnicker*, in the little leather sheath with the belt loop that he had the cobbler in town make for it after losing the traditional one that came with it. He always wore that little knife, which I found out later was the source of not a few jokes around town since *jagdnickers* are traditionally used to finish off a wounded deer by severing a vertebra in their necks—and my father didn't hunt. In fact, despite my father wearing lederhosen like the other men in our village he didn't do much of anything outdoors and certainly didn't display the level of skill with a knife that men from a rural community often possess. Most of the time, my father used that beautiful and wickedly sharp little knife to try and open walnuts, or to occasionally cut the wax seal on a bottle of brandy, which was a shame. In the right hands the stout little stag handle could be used to make that tapered little blade cut and stab through just about anything…anyhow…I could see my mother begin to become upset, any time she was upset she put her hands to her mouth and that is what she did now. Father staggered toward her but then tried to pass her to go into the kitchen. I thought for some reason that this was perhaps a good time to greet him, though of course, it would have been better if I had just gone back up the stairs quietly and sat next to my baby sister who by now was starting to become upset herself. "Papa! Merry Christmas!" I went to go over to him but just as I did so my mother tried to bar his way into the kitchen, the result being that he reached back, slowly, and with great focus, and then lurched forward and slapped her face with enough force to cause her to lose her balance and tumble down to the floor. I froze. He looked at me with a blank and hollow stare, and then stepped over my mother and entered the kitchen. I ran to her. She was crying but trying to make it look as if she wasn't crying. My father came back out of the kitchen, the fine silver dish in which my mother usually placed the goose in to serve on the table in his hands. My mother screamed his name as he forcefully flung it across the room with both arms, it slamming with a great crash against the wall next to the lit fireplace and knocking his framed certificate from von Bismarck off the wall in the process (I actually found out later that it wasn't a certificate personally from von Bismarck like I had been told, but rather his discharge papers from his service in the War of 1870 of which every participant received. It had a stamp of von Bismarck's signature after a paragraph thanking the volunteers of that conflict, nothing more). I shot to my feet, and instinctively dashed over to my wooden pull wagon that I had left out under the long table that was next to the kitchen door. I loved my little pull wagon, it was only about as big as a shoe and had four wooden wheels and a string which allowed me to pull it anywhere I wanted to. It was my favorite toy, we had spent endless hours the previous summer together as I pulled it through the meadow that was at the end of our road. At that very moment, I regretted more than anything in the world leaving it out under that table instead of putting it away back in my bedroom after I was done pulling it around the Christmas tree earlier. Too late! Father noticed my wagon and knocked me away as he hoisted it up from its hiding place beneath the table. I fell and landed with a crash in front of him, knocking my knee against the hard stone floor in the process, and pleaded with him as I stared up in confused horror. My mother cried out. My father reached back. I screamed. He looked down at us, staggered a bit, and then slammed my favorite wagon on the ground right in front of me. It landed with a crack, and as it did so the front left wheel broke off and shot across the floor and out of sight. I ran over to the wagon, scooped it up, and ran up the stairs to where my sister was rocking back and forth on her knees and sobbing. I fell down beside her and started to sob uncontrollably as well. Deep, frantic sobs as I too rocked back and forth, cradling by beloved toy that my father had just ferociously and wantonly attacked. I could hear my mother crying and my father crashing about in the kitchen, cursing aloud and threatening violence on everything in the house. I sobbed. I gasped for air. I needed to hide. I held my wagon. I couldn't catch my breath. I sobbed. I sobbed. I sobbed like a baby…

I had clay and various other unrecognizable debris stuck in the vomit all over the front of my tunic, and had soiled myself both front and back as well. Something must have struck my face while I was out since there was blood all matted in my hair and into my eyes, and my eyes were still watering. Laying on the ground in front of me was a portion of a driving band that just may have been what hit me in the face while I was out. Under other circumstances I would have gladly picked it up but at the moment I wasn't interested in souvenirs. I tried to stand but my right leg gave out immediately and I crashed back to my knees. There was smoke and dust hanging thickly in the air all around, and for the moment I couldn't hear anything but the whining and roaring of explosions in my ringing ears. I quickly felt myself over: My shirt was bloody but I think I vomited some of the blood up, since I didn't appear to have a chest wound. My right leg was bloody and had some metal barbs sticking out of it. But I still had both legs. And arms. Though my right arm was cut and was still bleeding. I started to come back to my senses, and the first thing I did next was crawl over to Lars. He was still lying face down more or less where I had thrown him, and I paused momentarily before I reached to turn him over. I knew all too well what his front side would look like if he had gotten hit again while I was out. I took a breath and turned him. His poor face! The shovel handle had done wicked work. His nose was clearly broken and his mouth a bloody mess, and his head was wet with blood as well. He seemed to be breathing. Okay. I didn't know what to do and I really can't explain why I did it, but I reached in and kissed him on the cheek. Twice. Just as I did so he choked and grunted back to life, spitting blood clots and clay everywhere as he gasped for air. I still had my Lars. I held him long enough for him to recognize me and then leaned him against the wall, turning then to our young friend Rolf. He had somehow rolled himself into a ball and was half buried with earth and rubble. I reached down and touched his shoulder. "Rolf? Rolf? Can you hear me?" He suddenly sprang to his knees and lunged at me, wrapping his arms around me and forcing me to tumble painfully over with him. He face was still twisted with terror: his eyes big and bulging, his mouth hung open while his bloody tongue lolled around all over like a madman's, and his flesh was as white as a ghost's. "Rolf! Are you alive? You're okay. You're okay." I laid him on the ground face up next to me and kind of looked him over. He seemed remarkably to be in one piece, minus some cuts and scrapes from being tossed around. Then I noticed it: it looked like he may have bitten off the end of his tongue. Yes, Oh God! He did. Poor guy. He was mewling like a lamb and occasionally letting out a high-pitched shriek. Hey, I could almost hear again! I turned back to Lars. "Lars! Are you alive? Can you hear me?" He went to speak but just ended up spitting out a mouthful of blood and muck instead. His mouth must have been hurt more than I had noticed. "It's okay, Lars, I'm here. We lived. We made it." I squeezed his hand and he squeezed it back. Now everything else started to come into focus.

All around us was a sea of human wreckage. Not everyone had been so fortunate as to have had a wall to shelter against. With difficulty, I rose on shaky legs, and was able to hobble a few steps if I favored my left leg. Everything around us was a mix of the same sad colors: Dull orange clay, blackened debris, pinkish-red flesh, and scorched white spots where rounds had incinerated whatever happened to be nearby when they landed. The air was acrid with cordite and the smells of carnage, and the more my eyes and ears began to adjust the more I was shocked by my surroundings. It was as if a great blacksmith had just finished pounding molten metal into pig iron, and now all that remained was the dross of his labors. My work detail had been rendered into the dross of a great furnace and now would have to be cleaned up as if it were wastage in a foundry. Few trees were left standing, and the ones that were had all been burned, stripped of their bark, and then adorned with strips of viscera and uniforms like tinsel. Everywhere were remnants of our work detail: A twisted portion of a wheelbarrow, a tool handle sticking out of the ground, the better portion of a draft horse with a surprisingly intact saddle still buckled around him, and parts of men. Arms without torsos, torsos without heads, heads without faces, and innards strewn about like streamers after a wedding. The human body is powerless against the awesome fury of artillery; it can kill with sheer energy alone and mangle flesh beyond recognition, sometimes vaporizing its victims without a trace. Unless one finds some form of shelter during a barrage it is purely by luck that he survives such an ordeal. My eyes kept jumping from one lump of man to another, hoping to land upon a comrade alive and in need of assistance. Oddly enough I wasn't able to make out where young Max had fallen because I was so disoriented, and also because his remains wouldn't have stood out amongst the gruesome tableau. Wait! A man crawls there. And another! Thank God we aren't alone. The groans of the wounded men and the wild cries of wounded horses are now beginning to fill the air, and just as it began to rise to a most pitiful howl I began to make out what sounded like shouts and the moving of motor vehicles from somewhere off to my left.

As it turns out, a second work detail was gathered and sent out not long after ours had departed, but was held back once the shelling of our position began. They were then met with several lorries of medics and rescue personnel coming from the other direction and then all sent foreword once the barrage lifted with the hopes of finding anything left of the position. I feebly raised my arm in the air as frantic men began fanning out to search the impact craters and loose clay for any survivors. Two men turned and saw me, and then my two companions, and yelled for a medic and stretchers. I collapsed back onto the ground as they rushed over to me, thankful that the army had thought to look after us after such a trying ordeal. What exactly happened next I'm not entirely sure: I remember being given a stimulant that burned my parched throat like fire when I swallowed it. I remember Rolf fussing as they tried to look him over and get him over to the lorries that now were going to double as ambulances to take us to the field hospital. I remember seeing that Lars needed to be carried on a stretcher, though I couldn't see why. And then I remember my head hitting the floor of the lorry with a thud as they laid me in it on a stretcher too. Apparently I was more hurt than I thought I was.

# Chapter Seven
# Die Franzosen

The men I suppose are all wild with joy this morning, or at least the ones that haven't given themselves the time for a proper reflection of the situation at hand at any rate. I hear all kinds of shouts and taunts being directed at the *boches* from all quarters, and the men at least in my section are strutting about with their chests out like roosters. But they are mostly young men. Young, and in some cases stupid, in most other cases naïve. I for one know better than to think that what occurred here yesterday is going to be a singular event, and that there won't be some sort of terrible retribution meted out on us in retaliation. *But when*? I will admit that the lack of response thus far has been intriguing. For starters, I had no idea that we had that kind of arsenal of artillery anywhere near this position, and the whole situation caught me completely off guard…it was about midafternoon, and I happened to be cleaning my pistol and sipping some *pinard* out of my battered and filthy tin cup when a breathless orderly appeared at the door to my dugout. Upon rising, I half expected to be handed an order to report on the results of my findings in regards to the lapse of security that had aided the German trench raid from the night before. Swallowing hard as I took the paper in hand (mostly because I hadn't even looked into the matter, and also because I was slightly drunk) I was astounded to read that I was to prepare my section for the delivery of a heavy barrage on the German lines, and the possible counter-barrage, later this afternoon. Incredible! To my knowledge there had not been any discussions of attacks in this sector, nor had I received any specific information at any of my daily briefings. Plus, I'd already been in the rear areas that morning and did not see any signs of activity or hear any rumors. What did this mean? We almost never just fire off heavies for the sake of it, they traditionally are fired to support a frontal attack, or in an attempt to repulse one. In any case, there wasn't time to send back for clarification. If the men in this section were even half as drunk as I was, then this was going be a challenging order to carry out in anything like a timely fashion.

I lined the men up in my section, and as usual extolled them for their continued vigilance and bravery in the face of such a determined enemy—this of course was said with the vivid memory still fresh in our minds of the young and inexperienced soldier that was killed this morning when he briefly exposed his head over the parapet to blow snot out of his nose. He hadn't even fully exhaled when a well-placed 8mm Mauser round smashed through his head and spattered his brains all over the trench behind him—yes, continued vigilance and bravery is what will win this war, etc., etc. I then explained what I knew to them about this impending barrage, and what to expect. Especially in regards to the potential counter-barrage and the potential for gas shells being mixed in. Every man was forced to put on his gas mask so that I or any other NCO in the section could inspect it. I then paired the men up, which makes it easier to locate and dig out comrades that become buried when a large shell lands nearby. The men were then dismissed to make peace and to prepare for whatever lay ahead in whatever manner of fashion they saw fit. I went back to my dugout, put my pistol back together and loaded it, and drank more *pinard.*

According to my wristlet, which I had thankfully thought to wind that morning, it was about 3 o'clock in the afternoon when I first heard, then saw several Nieuports head out toward the German lines. *Strange* I thought, those weren't bombers by any means, and are surely to be shot down if there's a flying circus about. In any case, soldiering as long as I have I took it as a sign that it was time to get ready. Ready for *anything.* I came out of my dugout, gas mask hung around my neck in its bag, canteen over my shoulder (full of Pinard, I hadn't had time to finish it and replace it with water), and a shovel in my hand which I leaned against the trench wall. I had even buckled the chin strap of my Adrian which I almost never did since I found the course leather strap to be irritating on my beard, and had further taken the time to put the new standard-issue canvas Adrian cover on it first with its pattern of dull colors splotched all over. The men got the hint from my grim appearance and began assuming ready and watchful positions, all with their gas masks at the ready and shovels close at hand. Good boys. There was even a young Corporal with a cut-down 75mm shell casing and a hammer, ready to sound the alarm if gas was detected. I had much to be proud of in my little section. Just then I noticed that the Nieuports were heading back to our lines, and as far as I could tell they weren't being followed. I was incredulous at the thought that they had flown over the German lines and back undetected, and further filled with wonder at their purpose.

Then it started.

Almost at once what seemed like a hundred guns went off from some unforeseen location far behind our lines. We all ducked down at the first roar, and stayed down with our Adrians pulled down tightly on our heads. But then as the barrage began to slow and separate into individual guns we all began to slowly rise and even to cautiously peer out over the parapet in front of us. "What's this?" I don't see any explosions! Sure, there was heavy smoke off on the horizon, but the guns were missing the German trenches in front of us! I quickly ordered the men off the parapet and back down into their defensive positions. Oh what a travesty! Not only were we expending hundreds if not thousands of artillery rounds and in the process giving away our strength and artillery position, but we were *missing!* I wrung my hands in disgust. I paced back and forth, outwardly expressing a steely confidence to my men but churning on the inside. What were they doing? If they ordered us to attack after this was over we'd surely be scythed down by their unscathed machine gunners before we were even halfway across no-man's land! Yet the bombardment went on, and on, the shots never landing any closer than the horizon. I took a long drink from my canteen, and checked my wristlet. The bombardment had been going on for almost forty-five minutes now, which as far as artillery barrages go was actually rather short. But the guns we were firing were *heavy.* No 75's here. These sounded like 105 Schneiders, or even heavy 220 mortars which shook the very earth when they fired. Every couple of seconds just by luck two or more pieces would go off more or less at once, and the report and subsequent wave of energy through the earth was strong enough, even at this distance, to rumble your innards and shake the trench around us. After a particularly strong shockwave in which I stumbled a little as it passed, I peered back into my dugout to see that most of my personal effects were now strewn all over the floor. Great. Then, just as abruptly as it began, it began to subside. Our big guns began to go off individually, with enough time in between for us to make out the faint sound of the explosion on the other end. Well, whatever it was that they hit was surely destroyed by now, but what *was* it that they hit? It certainly wouldn't do us much good if all of this had only served to churn up their rear areas, since that would only kill officers and orderlies of which there were always a steady stream of qualified replacements. No, when big guns were fired they needed to kill large groups of fighting men, or at least to destroy important equipment or infrastructure to be considered effective. One hour and twenty minutes. The bombardment had essentially lifted. As a precaution I walked over to the Corporal with the gas alarm and told him to ring it, just in case. The loud peals of the hammer against the brass sent men into a frantic pantomime as they all struggled to put on their gas masks and to then try to calm down and breathe slowly so that they didn't become light-headed and pass out from lack of air. Okay, the barrage was definitely over. With a lump in my throat, I carefully peered over the parapet—nothing. Nothing! If there was any activity in the German lines it is all below ground: nothing on the surface stirred. After an agonizing thirty minutes, I instructed the men to pull their masks off but remain on guard for anything, which they gladly did, many of them falling to the trench floor gasping for fresh air once they had the dreadful things off.

And on guard for anything we remained. Right through the afternoon and into the evening. Nothing. Were they all dead? Nonsense! Around seven o'clock an orderly appeared with tidings of dinner for the men. Cold rations, but food nonetheless. We ate at our posts, rifles and gas masks at the ready. Still nothing. As it grew dark I forbade the men to smoke their pipes or light candles (which was a useless and sure to be ignored order, as everyone knows that if a French soldier cannot smoke he will not fight or stand his post) as if by doing so the Germans would suddenly discover the location of our trench— the same one they had duly raided last night—but this was military protocol. At nine o'clock, I ordered the men to stand down, shook out a double guard of sentries and posted Corporals with gas alarms, told the men they could smoke as long as they shielded their cigarettes (they'd all already been smoking for hours) and retired for the night.

But that was yesterday, and today was a new day. One begins to consciously note when you've lived through another night up here on the line and all the more so when something happens that is out of the ordinary. So yes, this was another day. It was a gloomy day: the sky was gray and sullen and it smelled like rain was in the offing. Good thing this little stunt of ours was yesterday and not today since this is bad weather for flying. That is, assuming that those mystery Nieuports had anything to do with the bombardment. The aforementioned taunts and verbal jabs at the *boches* by the men continues unabated as the inevitable trench gossip begins to make the rounds. Many of the young men who haven't experienced worse undoubtedly are bragging about the ferocity of the bombardment, and I've personally heard several references to how "they must all be dead" and how "we can't wait to walk over and root through their belongings for souvenirs." Yes, yes. Young men. Young, naïve, and stupid.

# Chapter Eight
# Les Allemands

Rain. I think it's raining. Yes, that must be rain. With difficulty, I rose slightly and turned a little toward the window down the hall from our row of cots. I had guessed correctly; the dirty little window was rain-streaked. I laid back down into my cot and thought about what it meant to rain. Mud. That was the first thought. Endless mud. Mud that ruined boots and fouled weapons, mud that filled dugouts and ruined food, mud that drowned men and rats alike. Yet as rain made mud which made life miserable, the rain also let us all live another day. When it rained, all of Europe was forced to hold its breath and wait. Rain made it impossible to fire artillery or machine-guns unless absolutely necessary, made it impossible to get aero-planes off the ground at all, and made mounting assaults of any kind a fruitless venture. Yes when it rained all of Europe was forced to wait for the skies to clear so that the cheerful sun breaking through the clouds could signal that it was time for the normal killing to resume. Today was going to be a very quiet, soggy day out on the lines.

But it was never quiet around here. Someone was always moaning or sobbing, or jabbering to themselves, and there were always nurses and orderlies coming and going. New patients were constantly being brought in, and occasionally dead ones were being wheeled out. Rolf's cot was next to mine, on my left, and he was almost always making some sort of moaning or whimpering noise. Plus the orderlies were always checking on him and the state of his cot due to his nearly constant bed wetting. Lars was on the cot to my right though for a while a ghastly wounded soldier separated us. He was a poor mangled thing, with no legs and bandages over most of his body. I never heard him speak for the brief time that we were neighbors: today they wheeled him out and moved Lars over next to me of which I am eternally grateful. The bombardment has been a terribly trying ordeal for the German army in this sector and the casualties and injuries have been heavy. I can see with my own eyes how fortunate the three of us are to have lived through it as intact as we are. Everywhere are amputees and mangled men, the sights of which have begun to creep into my already disturbed sleep with a frightening regularity. A poor soldier across the walkway between our cots has had the majority of his face torn away, yet lives and breathes still I know not how. He receives nearly constant attention from the nurses and even doctors, who frequently remove his bandages to inspect the damage and to wipe his wounds. This is a hideous spectacle, made all the more so by his unintelligible garbles and moans as they do so. I wish they would move him, or put up a cloth curtain of some sort to separate him from the rest of us…my how I've become callous. I should say, I wish that he still had a face and was just wounded in some other way. Wait what am I saying? Rather, I wish that none of us were here lying here mangled and that none of us were wounded at all. I mean…oh forget it. I don't know what I mean. Of course I wish that none of this had happened, but if one is to play that game then you'd have to undo a great deal of nasty things indeed before life could be pleasant again and that would be maddening.

Suddenly, the door at the end of the hall opens and an orderly appears, pushing a large cart. He has apparently brought some sort of food, and appears to have a little chart that he is checking as he makes his way down the line of cots. I imagine that the chart has helpful information on it such as: "Who still has a mouth/face and so can still chew food versus those that do not, who has received a serious stomach wound and who therefore should not be fed, and who is likely to die soon and so therefore is not worth feeding." He is working his way toward us and so I thought that I had better rouse my companions so that they can eat if they'd care to. "Rolf, hey Rolf. Do you want some food? Are you hungry? A man is coming with food."

He turns over in his cot and looks at me with his doe eyes and blank stare. "Do you want food Rolf?" He smiles at me, and then sits up in his cot like a puppy. "Lars, Lars, are you awake? Lars it looks like we might be getting some food, are you hungry?" He stirs, stretches out, and slowly rolls over to face me. "Food? Does it look good? Tell the man that I'll have a schweinshaxe and a weissbier, and to go heavy on the cabbage on the side." Ah my Lars, yet not quite my Lars. I, of course, laughed as heartily at that as mirth in this setting would allow, but he merely smirked and then sunk back to his pillow, the smile quickly fading from his face. I know he was in a lot of pain, and I'm sure it hurt to talk and would indeed hurt to eat, but he was not himself. "I'll ask him Lars, and I'll get a round of Underbergs to wash it all down with!" At this he didn't even crack a smile. The shovel handle had done beastly work to his face. His nose was broken and his left eye was swollen almost shut, both his lips were split open, and he had several internal mouth injuries which included a few missing teeth. He more than likely would never look quite the same again, which was hard, since he was so handsome when we first met. I suppose it was nothing compared to losing a face, but it was still hard to bear for an attractive man.

The orderly has stopped at the foot of our three cots, and is checking our charts. The information written on them must be quite generalized because he hardly gave them a glance before setting each of them back on their little pegs and then turning to address us. "Time to eat. You should try to eat, even a little. It will help you heal, and then you will be able to leave and let someone else use your cot." His lack of empathy for our situation was astounding. "I will go ahead and prepare three trays." In a blink of an eye, he had taken three small bowls and ladled a hot soup into them from a large lidded steel pot. He then set each on its own tray, plunked a large spoon down next to each along with a dirty-looking napkin, and then placed each tray on one of our three cots. He then rummaged around in a large cloth sack and produced three very stale looking pieces of dark bread which he distributed, and then was off to feed the rest of the room. All of us I suppose were hungry enough and so we each in turn slid our trays back and tried as best we could to get propped up and comfortable with our one battered and deteriorated hospital pillow. The bowl contained a thin, grayish soup that looked and smelled as if it had potatoes as a main ingredient. There were little bits of things floating around in it too but long experience as a soldier told me not to investigate too closely what those pieces might be but just to ignore them as long as they didn't move. I tore a chunk off of my piece of bread and dunked it in the soup, only to find that small insects were left floating around in the bowl after I had done so. I supposed that this food was to help us want to leave and "let someone else use our cot," but in reality, it's no worse than anything else that we've been living off of and so I tucked in, as did my two companions.

But there was no escaping that it wasn't good, and that someone had added a generous dose of salt to it in an effort to either help rehydrate us or to try and cover the foul taste of the water that was used to make it. In any case, I could see that Lars was wincing and struggling after every spoonful that he placed in his mouth. Poor guy, it probably stings something terrible on all his cuts. Rolf was struggling too, but for a different reason. From what I could gather, he had bitten off a rather large portion of his tongue during the bombardment, and maybe even gnawed the inside of his mouth as well. Now he could barely communicate (though he had barely tried) and more than likely had difficulty tasting or even swallowing. In any case, he was making a mess of his bowl of soup. Every time he put a spoonful of soup in his mouth he would leave his lips parted and then sort of slurp or gargle it down his throat. The end result was that he was both making a mess by dribbling soup out of the corners of his mouth and emitting the most disturbing and loudly grotesque eating noises in the process. I admit that this was unpleasant, but what in this setting wasn't? I looked over at him just as he had slurped down another spoonful, and when our eyes met he sheepishly smiled and then wiped the soup off of his face—or rather tried to wipe his face but instead just smeared the gruel around with his filthy napkin. He then took another spoonful in his mouth and gargled in down when "Fuck!"

"God dammit!"

"Can you fucking stop making that horrible noise when you eat?"

Lars suddenly flew into a rage over the eating sounds that Rolf was making. "I can't stand the sound of you eating, you're disgusting!" I just put my spoon down and stared at Lars. How incredibly cruel of him! He of all people should know how hard it is to eat with a mouth injury, and on top of that he himself was eating rather noisily. This is not my Lars: A joke about it maybe, but he'd never lash out at someone like he just did now. I turned to Rolf to find that he had put his spoon down and was staring at me. As our gaze met a large tear welled in his eye and then rolled down his cheek, and his upper lip began to tremble. I immediately recognized in him the hurt little boy at the dinner table and with it came an instant hot rush of self-loathing and anger. I felt my face flush and my brow furrow.

"What the fuck, Lars? Can't you leave the guy alone? He bit his fucking tongue off during the…" Just as I was about to say 'bombardment' and then undoubtedly start an argument with the man that I'd never before wanted to argue with a crash from across the room stopped us all in our tracks.

An orderly had been assigned to each soldier that could still eat but was otherwise unable to feed himself. In the row across from us and a little further down to the right was a soldier who had to have both of his arms amputated in order to save his life. I had worked into my waking routine to never look at him, which was easy since he was close to the man who had had his face torn off. I never looked at him because he just laid in his cot all day, awake, and stared the most hawkish stare at the ceiling. His face was so twisted and angry that it made my injuries of a sprained and lacerated knee with debris penetration, lacerated arm, lacerated neck, and internal bleeding seem so minor as to be embarrassing. Once he even met my gaze, and before I could look away he had bored two holes through me with his furious black eyes. I only could look away and shudder to myself after, and secretly hope that he would be moved away for one reason or another. I suppose it was to be understood since I honestly didn't know how he was going to live his life without arms, and I know myself that I would be furious, but nevertheless his presence was unsettling. For his feeding, he was sitting propped up in his cot with his pillow bunched behind him, and the orderly was seated on a small folding chair in between his cot and the next. What must have occurred is that the orderly, who had the tray of soup and bread on his lap, went to feed the wounded soldier a spoonful of soup but had callously not bothered to check the temperature of the soup before doing so. Apparently the soup on the other side of the room was very hot, because when the orderly went to spoon some soup into the soldier's mouth he burned him with the steaming liquid. What happened next was appalling.

The soldier immediately spit the hot soup out everywhere while simultaneously thrashing his legs and shouting out in agony. This caused the orderly to jolt in his seat and to spill the bowl of very hot soup all over his own lap. This caused the orderly to cry out and to jump to his feet in agony, which knocked over his chair and sent the empty tray flying. Now both the soldier and the orderly were thrashing about generally and cursing both one another and their luck in general, when all of a sudden due to his violent leg thrashing the soldier became unbalanced and slid sideways out of his cot and fell heavily to the floor. How humiliating! Now orderlies were rushing over from all directions, some picking up the wounded soldier while others tried to clean up the mess. All the while the orderly with the burnt lap went sprinting off toward the operating room to no doubt assess the damage and to clean himself up. What a sad, frustrating, and disturbing display that all was. I was angry for the armless soldier at the humiliation he just faced, and could only shudder to think what humiliations he'll face in the future…

"What a fucking mess!" Lars chortled at the situation as he tore off a chunk of bread and dipped in his soup. "I wonder if that orderly burned his penis. Hey Rolf, Rolf, go see if that guy burned his penis." Lars then took a big bite of soggy bread and sort of laughed to himself as he chewed (rather loudly, I may add) and pretended not to notice how disgusted I was or how hurt Rolf was. I am starting to really become concerned that something has changed in my Lars. He has always been a cocky, devil-may-care kind of guy with a very sharp sense of humor, but he was never before cruel for cruelty's sake. In fact, he always seemed to reserve his most cutting comments for those that deserved them, such as that lout Jürgen back up at the front. I suppose that we all have a right to be angry at having been bombarded and injured like we were, but to me at least this wasn't grounds to become a bully—especially since all of us in this room faced the same terrible ordeal and so therefore were bonded in a way by the experience. I had just made my mind up to say something to him when a familiar voice came to us from around the corner.

"Excuse me. I'm looking for any of the above names on this list. Do any of them look familiar? I understand that all of these soldiers here in this field hospital were involved in the same incident." I knew that voice anywhere. Before I could even cry out, I heard the tell-tale crunch of hobnailed boots turn toward my way and thump across the wooden floor of the infirmary. It was Corporal Pangloss!

"Ah! Yes. There you are. Kurt, Lars, and who's this fellow here?"

"Rolf! This is Rolf. He had joined up with us just as we were heading out to the detail. Some timing huh?" At that I shot Rolf a look and a smile, which he returned with a schoolboy smirk. "Rolf! Yes of course, here you are my list. Okay, one, two, three…" His voice trailed off as he studied the careworn yet still official looking piece of paper he had in his hand. His brow was furrowed, and by the way his eyes darted up and down the page in front of him I could tell that he had hoped to find more soldiers alive from our section. As he stood there with his piece of paper he shook his feldmuntz a few times with his other hand to get some of the water off of it, and then brushed his tunic off as best as he could before sitting down in the folding chair at the base of my cot. "Well it is exceptionally fine to find you three here and in such good health. Now that I've laid eyes on you three I can process the appropriate paperwork to recognize your wounding, as well as the paperwork to authorize your time off. Oh yes, you three will be receiving some leave. I can't at this time promise that I can get you a ticket all the way home to see your folks, the railroads being pressed as they are, but you all will have some time away from the front I can tell you that." A big smile spread across all three of our faces, though at that moment I could already tell that all three of us were thinking of different ways we'd like to rest once we were away from that field hospital and the front lines. "How have things been at the front? Did you ever get to lead that raid that you were talking about before we left for that detail?"

I was curious to see who would have been picked to go in our absence. "No, the raid was cancelled for that evening on account of the unexpected bombardment which honestly caught everyone by surprise. Since the bombardment a Jasta of Albatros Ds has been flying constant sorties over the length of the front in order to prevent any more reconnaissance by the French air wing and to do some looking of our own. Our fighters have even done a little strafing of their trenches from what I understand, which I'm sure has been unpleasant for the little blue frog-eaters. All in all it's been a tense few days of wait-and-see."

At this, Rolf looked at me with a puzzled look on his face, but before he could even ask Pangloss turned to him and said, "A Jasta is a group of fighter planes, and the Albatros D is one our newest and most powerful bi-planes." That's our Pangloss. He was practically a father to us for all the right reasons (and a few of the wrong) and always seemed to know what needed to be said and how to say it. I always felt that after the war he should meet a girl and start a family straight away.

"Well gentlemen, any more questions? If not, I need to get back up to the front so that I can process this information. From what the doctor has told me, you three will be out of here in another few days, and I want to make sure that the right paperwork is waiting for you when you get back to your dugouts."

At this, Lars piped up for the first time since Pangloss' unexpected arrival. "Hey, you said that we weren't going to be going back up to the front for a while after we get out of this hell-hole. What gives Corporal?" I was a little shocked at Lars' tone, and the way that he addressed Pangloss. Even though he was our friend, it was still disrespectful to address an NCO by his rank. Despite the verbal rebuff, however, Pangloss just smiled and turned to Lars without batting an eye.

"Well Lars, first off, that's *Sergeant* to you. As soon as that big bombardment began I immediately put our section in a ready position to receive an attack, and once that was accomplished I also organized one of the first relief missions to be sent back to find you all. It was felt that my handling of the situation was above average and so was therefore grounds for an elevation in rank." We hadn't even noticed his collar due to how dark feldgrau became when it got wet, but he'd finally been promoted! "And yes, I did say that you would be relieved from front line duties for a time. But tell me Lars, how would you like to go on leave with only the clothes on your back? Surely you'd prefer to return to your dugout and pack a bag for your week off." At this, he rose in his seat and brushed his tunic smooth with his hands and then clapped his legs to settle his trousers. NCOs are always concerned with their appearances. "If there's nothing further, then I must take my leave of you three. Rest up and eat, and I will see you three again in a few days."

As he went to turn and walk down the row of cots toward the door I stopped him. "Sergeant Pangloss?" He stopped and looked back at me.

"Congratulations on the promotion, you deserve it." At that, he smiled at me and then walked off through the infirmary and out back into the rain, his heavy hobnailed boots crunching on the wooden floor all the way out. "Way to kiss his ass Kurt." I just ignored Lars as I slunk back into the pillow on my cot and listened to the rain on the roof of the infirmary.

# Chapter Nine
# Die Franzosen

Today I awoke with a start and a familiar stink in my nostrils. Rain. I knew it must have been raining because water was dripping down from the ceiling of my dugout onto my face, which had provided the impetus for my rather abrupt rising. Once awake, my suspicions were confirmed from the distinctive smell that filled my lungs as I inhaled my first gasp of air for the day. Rain. Rain turned our world into a disgusting quagmire; a mixture of mud, clay, human and animal waste, and corpses, and it smelled horrendously. I struggled to muster the strength to even get out of my cot for I knew my dugout was flooding, yet I could already hear the men hard at work attempting to deal with the situation out in the trench and besides, I knew that soon they would be wanting guidance in their endeavors. So I carefully pulled the blankets back as to not let them touch the ground and spun ever so gingerly around into a sitting position to assess my personal situation. My boots were just where I had left them, at the foot of my cot, and were sitting in about 5 centimeters of water. Dammit anyway. I was thankful at the moment that I had at least a duck-boarded floor to my hovel, but nonetheless the water was cold as I stood up in it, and the mud that squeezed between the boards was foul and oily. Luckily my little tobacco tin was still sealed and dry, as was my handy trench lighter, but unfortunately it appears as if I had left my pipe out where it could get wet and as a result it now was in no state to smoke. Dammit anyway. I knew I had a package of commissary cigarettes in my uniform jacket pocket however, which in the end provided me some comfort as I carefully assembled the 'clean' uniform that I was to wear for the day and dressed myself as best as I could. One of the more unpleasant experiences of a morning like this is that of trying to squeeze wet and swollen feet into wet and shrunken boots, and this morning's efforts were no exception. In fact, I found myself a little winded from the proceedings, and in need of a tot of Pinard to re-center my momentum. With cigarette smoked and cup drained, I put my Adrian on (which was useless for keeping one's head dry on account of the center vent, though with the new canvas cover installed it was marginally better) and grabbed my shovel before pushing through the door and out into the muck and grime of my little stretch of our foreword line.

Ah, and what a sight to greet one's eyes! Men up and down the line covered in mud as they took turns attempting to shovel out our flooded trench, while others tried in vain to scoop up buckets full of stinking brown water and toss them out toward the German lines. To make matters worse a steady cold rain was falling, which quickly soaked through my tunic and into my uniform underneath. That, and my first steps into the trench brought water and mud up passed my ankles, and it wasn't long before my boots were completely waterlogged and heavy. Dammit anyway. Today was going to be long and disgusting. Though at least I wouldn't have to worry about the boches today since weather like this automatically calls a time-out on the killing, which was a welcome break for me. These last few days have been trying, the boches lashed out rather sharply after our artillery pounded their rear areas a little while back. In response, they brought up a flying circus that was apparently powerful enough to suppress our own aircraft, since they have been able to strafe our front-line areas with machine guns and pepper us with flechettes seemingly at will. Granted, this all has caused relatively few actual casualties in my section, but was nonetheless terrifying since it kept us pinned down in our holes for the duration and kept the men glancing skyward lest they catch a steel dart through their helmet. What has been worse, however, has been that it seems as if they've brought up one of their horrible little minenwerfers somewhere opposite us as well, since not a few bombs have been tossed our way rather randomly over the last few days which have killed and wounded dozens. It must be a small one too since just as quickly as the firing begins it stops, only to start up again further down the line. They must be able to manhandle it from section to section and in that way keep us guessing as to when and where it will strike next. There has been some desultory firing from our lines in response but thus far our efforts have proven to be in vain; we possess no weapon capable of tossing a bomb that far in my section, and when we call for artillery our 75's seem to fire right over their heads. The boches always seem to be one step ahead of us when it comes to killing and always kept their morning hate interesting.

But not today. Today will be a day of misery and toil against an enemy that cannot be beaten; mother nature. Just now I hear commotion off to my right. It appears as if a small section of the trench is caving in due to the sides washing out, and I immediately cry out orders to the effect that men are needed to prevent this from tuning into a full-out cave in. "You and you, quickly grab those boards and prop them against the sagging wall. You and you, run and fetch more duck boards from the area just behind us where extras are kept. You and you, bring your shovels and help shore up that wall etc. etc." And then the most dreadful of things happened; a mostly decomposed shape of a man began to emerge from the caving-in wall of the trench, face first to be exact, and his sudden arrival proved to be as shocking as it was abhorrent. Immediately all work comes to a halt as men fall ill about the scene and add more disgusting materiel to our flooded trench to be shoveled out. Only the stout-hearted and/or the callous can experience something such as this and not be effected, and I suppose I must lay somewhere between the two since I'm managing thus far to keep my pinard down as the situation is unfolding. As per usual when something of this nature occurs the men now are forming a wide circle around the corpse and refusing to continue to work until something is done. That 'something' usually means that a hasty burial party must be got up and put to the task of removal. But right now I do not have the luxury of taking the time for such measures, as my foreword trench is threatening to collapse around me if the shoveling and shoring doesn't resume in a timely fashion. My Sergeant's stripes whisper in my ear, and nudge me a little toward what I already know I must do. As I rush over to our visitor from the crypt my men of course all take another step back, and I can almost hear them gasp as I pull my handkerchief from my pocket and tie it around my mouth and nose like a highwayman. Without hesitation I drove my long-handled shovel into the mud behind him and started prying back and forth in the hopes that this would dislodge him and allow us to heave him over the parapet. Not so, unfortunately. As it became quickly apparent his uniform was about the only thing keeping him together in his state, and my vigorous prying was just enough to get him to go to pieces. To my—and to everyone else who witnessed it—everlasting horror his upper torso became dislodged and spilled out into the muck that was quickly filling the bottom of the trench, disgorging the remnants of his entrails and an entire colony of pus-colored worms in the process. That did it. Now all work completely stopped as men began to flee in all directions to try and escape the scene while I stood trembling, alone, with a rotten torso at my feet and the soft rain coming down on my helmet…

After thoroughly voiding the contents of my stomach and ruining a good handkerchief in the process, I felt weak and hot and needed a moment to clear my nostrils of the reek that had enveloped me. As I was only a few dozen meters from my dugout I returned to briefly smoke another cigarette and sip a little more pinard in the quiet of my room. After gathering myself, I again put on my Adrian—completely full of water this time—and grabbed my shovel as I headed back out the door and did not let the irony of repeating the exact thing I had just done a little over an hour ago escape me. That was life on the front line; the same uncomfortable, monotonous life went on, day after day, punctuated here and there by horrible little scenes of violence and gore. As I turned back toward my unfinished business and set my jaw against what I must do I was pleasantly surprised to see that several Caporals from my section had stepped in to try and deal with the gruesome task that I had begun. In fact, I arrived just as they were freeing his lower half, his upper half having already been heaved over the edge of the trench (toward the Germans, of course). This gave me heart and also reminded me that I needed to regain control of the situation, and so I again bellowed out a series of orders directing the men back to work and in which specific ways they were to do so. Miraculously the cave-in that had started and which had uncovered our fallen friend had not worsened despite all of the prying and scooping that was needed to remove him. Quickly then we were able to gain the upper hand and shore up the sagging wall, and before long the section was repaired. Granted the experience was nothing short of awful, and it left a rather large quantity of unpleasantries in our trench that now needed to be bucketed out, but I was very thankful that it wasn't any worse. Had the trench completely collapsed we would be dangerously exposed to German fire once the storm broke and the daily wastage resumed.

But for now the storm held, and in doing so assured us of a long and muddy day full of chasing potential cave-ins and bucketing out filth and slime. Luckily, and thankfully, the rest of the day proved to be far less eventful than the morning's proceedings, and passed as a series of repeated motions and aching muscles. That evening's 'meal' consisted of iron rations for myself and the men as the bringing up of hot rations in these conditions was impossible, and passed with little comment and even less mirth. As the evening's sentries were being posted the rain mercifully tapered off to a mist before finally stopping altogether, and a low fog began to settle over no-man's land and our rear areas behind us. We could hear the rats scurrying around in the mud out in front of our line, no doubt feeding upon the freshly uncovered remains that were washed up over the course of the day, and I swore that I could hear the Germans across the way as they smoked and talked and tried to shake off the damp. I was probably just hearing our own men in the trench as it ran out to the left and right of us, but the fog played tricks on my hearing and made me not a little uneasy as our visibility was steadily being reduced. I could see it on the men's faces as well, and I did my best to assure them that despite the fog it would be impossible for raiding tonight on account of the mud, as any men who crawled out into no-man's land at the moment were liable to drown. Just the same, I warned them to keep alert and to shield their trench lighters when lighting their pipes and cigarettes and to keep their chatter to a low minimum. I myself was actually feeling so uneasy that I slung my Lebel over my shoulder before I headed out to walk my rounds up and down the line, which is something I rarely did and something that immediately caught the attention of the men in my section and told them without further ado that I was serious. Tonight would be an uncomfortable one for everyone, though I took heart that the rain and mud did not discriminate between belligerents.

# Chapter Ten
# Les Allemands

Today, finally, was to be the day. Over the last week orderlies came to work with us at given intervals to make sure that we could walk and somewhat function on our own. I for one had a great deal of difficulty trying to stand and to get around at first, so much so in fact that it was ordered that I be provided with a rude crutch of sorts for the time being. My right knee was still very tender and stiff and I was really unable to put much weight on it at all at first, but I was determined to build myself up and to get out of this hospital and so I took quite a few walks up and down the aisle in front of our cots with my crutch. Lars even came with me a time or two and was even pleasant on occasion, helping me along when I needed it and commenting on how strong I was becoming. His face was starting to heal a bit too and I told him as much. The swelling was going down around his eye and the bruising was fading, and his blue eyes were no longer bloodshot. We were starting to look more like a pair of pals who'd lost a pub-brawl than a couple of unlucky frontschwein who'd been caught in the wrong place at the wrong time.

And today was to finally be the day. Rolf, Lars and I were provided with some very rough and ill-fitting clothes that consisted of gray civilian trousers and a woolen field shirt, which struck me as odd since the clothes would readily assist us if we considered attempting to desert on our way back up to the lines. But that didn't seem to cross our minds at the moment. As we stood in line in the small office at the front of the hospital I could see a desk with an orderly seated at it up ahead. There was some small talk amongst us soldiers and a lot of shuffling while we were slowly processed and moved up toward where he was stamping and signing away. As the wounded soldiers were being filed past him each would pause before his desk to answer a few questions, and once he was satisfied he would motion for the newly processed soldier to head toward the door at the front of the room. This entire process reminded me of how I got here in the first place; my recruitment went almost exactly the same way and if I remember correctly I may have even been asked some of the very same questions. Anyway. I had to assist Rolf once it was his turn since he was still having such a tough time communicating, though to his credit he was finally beginning to try and speak again. The desk orderly didn't really seem to care either way as long as Rolf signed his own paperwork, which he did. Soon enough we took our first steps outside in weeks and breathed in full lungs of fresh air, freshly signed and stamped release papers clutched in our hot little hands. Was it exhilarating? Not necessarily. It had been rainy lately and so the world that greeted us was pretty damp and dull, though at least it wasn't raining now and there was a breeze (which admittedly felt good) which would in time help dry things out. "Hey Lars, does any of this look familiar? I don't remember any of this. I don't even know where we are."

I meant that too, I was really disoriented. "Beats me. I think we all must have been out cold or something when we were brought in. I couldn't tell you where we are or for that matter which direction we even need to go in to get back to the front."

I then turned to Rolf, who was gazing around in wonder as if he had never been to France before. "Hey, Rolf, are you okay? Do you recognize where we are?"

"No" is all he said, and I wasn't really sure at the moment which of my two questions this was the answer to. In any case just then a large and rather tired-looking lorry came wheezing around the bend, a little ways up the road from us and turned in our direction. It looked as if it wouldn't be long now before we'd know which direction we'd need to go to get back up to the trenches…

The lorry ride wasn't much to speak of. It was cramped, two men sat side-by-side on either side of it while some men elected to stand down the center aisle. It was ponderously slow and cruelly jarring as we ambled along over the rutted and worn road that led us back to our lines. After a time, we noticed another lorry far behind us which told me that there must be some sort of circuit that rotated up to the front like a great conveyor. No one really spoke much, partly because it was hard to hear over the roar of the engine but also because there wasn't much to say. As we got closer and closer to our lines the scene began to spread out before us on either side of the truck. Slowly the trees began to disappear, followed by the birds and then the grass. The distinction between the road and the fields began to blur as well, and soon enough all was brown and gray and in motion around us. Files of marching men, staff cars puttering this way and that, mounted officers trotting by on tired and mud-caked horses, and then finally, we stopped. "This is it?" I said as I turned toward Lars and shrugged my shoulders.

"How do they know that we have arrived at the right point?"

Something that should never be questioned is German efficiency, especially when the movement of men and materiel is in question. One only need to review the railroad operation that brought the army to the frontiers in 1914 to understand precisely what I mean. Sure enough the moment we were squeezed out of the lorry and down the little wooden set of steps we all recognized this as a marshalling depot that led directly back to our front-line trenches. In fact, I was almost certain that this is where we marched through on our way up to the 'construction duties' that landed us in the field hospital in the first place. If it was, all traces of those lush woods are now gone, as was any real evidence of the stollen we were supposed to be building. I suppose the bombardment took care of that, though at the moment I didn't see any craters either. "Attention men! Form a line here, and be ready to present your release papers when called upon! You will be placed in groups and led back up to your units by NCO's at given intervals. Do not leave this area for any reason!" It had been a while since we'd been barked at, and I found myself almost squinting at the jarring words being fired at us by the oberleutnant that was stalking back and forth in front of us. A group of NCOs were off a little ways ahead all standing around a tree stump and smoking, and I supposed this was to be the pool of leaders that would be bringing us back to our lines. I kept scanning their faces, hoping to find Pangloss amongst them but to no avail.

We weren't milling around long before the lorry that we spotted on the road lumbered up and disgorged its contents of men into the throng that was growing around us. Many of the men getting off were still bandaged around their heads and some even had arms in slings. I thought to myself how sorry a spectacle it presented, and thought almost aloud how these men must surely be on their way to some sort of medical leave or even discharge and not back up into the lines. As I turned my attention back to my comrades, I noticed Lars had wandered off to another group of soldiers but was just now returning, and was wearing the best smirk his still unhealed face could muster. "How about a smoke, Kurt? I just traded a ring I found in the hospital for two packs of cigarettes." As he was speaking he was already peeling back the paper wrapper on one of the packs and starting to work two cigarettes out from the bunch.

"Sure! Wow, it's been forever since I've had a smoke." It had been, too. "But what about Rolf? Hey Rolf, want a cigarette?" Rolf came walking over and smiled at me like a boy and held out his hand.

At this, Lars' face suddenly darkened, and as he narrowed his eyes at me he took a step back from us two. "Who the hell are you, giving away my smokes? Does this look like a Red Cross canteen?" Once again Lars flashed the new nasty side of his personality at me and flew into a rage over something seemingly innocent or trivial.

"Oh for Christ's sake, Lars, don't be such an asshole. Fine, if you won't give him one he can have mine."

"Oh no you don't. We're all going to have a nice smoke together. You, me, and little Rolfy." At this, he thrust a cigarette into each of our hands and then pulled out a small tin of matches, striking one off the side of his boot for us all to share. As we three leaned in to light our cigarettes I wrinkled my nose at him as if to call him an asshole again, but rather than respond in anger he roared into a chuckle and then took a long drag before trying several times to blow a smoke ring over his head. Rolf looked a little puzzled, like he had either never smoked a cigarette before or had never been called Rolfy, and in either case he seemed to be enjoying both. I took a long drag and let my thoughts begin to wander; "What the hell is wrong with my friend? Why is he becoming so unpredictable and quick to anger? And where the hell did he 'find' a ring while we were in the hospital?" Just as I was beginning to shudder at the thought of him slipping a ring off of a sleeping soldier's finger I was snapped back into reality by the intervention of helpful unteroffizer.

"You three! Get over here and join this file. You will be leaving for the front lines now!" Apparently we three were to be the last of this group because no sooner had we gotten into line that we started to march single file back up toward the front. Not too much of a relaxing smoke I'm afraid, but at least we weren't ordered to extinguish them which was nice I suppose. Lars was in front of me and was puffing away like mad on his cigarette, only to then light another one with the dying embers of his first. I couldn't imagine that he was nervous, given that we had all been promised some leave by Pangloss when he visited us in the field hospital, but then again I guess I was feeling a little uneasy at the moment myself. Actually, as the open area around us began to close in, and to then finally constrict into a trench around us as we entered it I suddenly got the sensation that I was being swallowed up by a great snake. The rhythmic bobbing of the men's heads as we navigated the trench line that was getting deeper and narrower as we inched closer to danger only helped to intensify this feeling. Suddenly I found myself beginning to quietly panic, and was just starting to eye the sides of the trench for a footing in which I could use to make my escape when I was abruptly brought back to reality by my cigarette. Or rather, by my cigarette burning down to my fingers. I had forgotten about it, and now I had a tiny little burn to remember it by. As I was blowing on my finger and cursing to myself a feeble little voice came from behind me. "Helmets? Helmets?" It was Rolf, and what I think he was trying to say made a good point. We should've all been issued helmets before they sent us back up to the front. Despite the trench line we were in, all the French would have to do is land a shell even remotely close to us and half of us would go down with head wounds.

Just then our line suddenly stopped, and with the sudden stop in motion came the rising feeling panic in me again. I reached out and touched Lars on the shoulder. "Hey, everything okay? Can you see why we have stopped?" (A famous soldier technique is to ask those around you if they are okay when actually you yourself are nervous or scared).

"Yeah, I'm fine. I can't really see what's going on but I wished they'd just get it over with. I'd like to actually *get* to our line before the sun goes down." (From his response, I gathered that Lars was feeling uneasy too, since another famous soldier technique is to seem bored or impatient when in actuality you are feeling nervous or vulnerable). I was about to check on Rolf when we got started again, and we hadn't gone more than 100 meters before we made a sharp right followed by a sharp left. Now we were in it. The beginning of the series of front-line trenches. Now the trench began to zig-zag as we went forward, and barbed wire began to sprout out over our heads. Funny, I didn't actually think that we were that close to the front yet, since things were still so very quiet. It was a quiet war today I guess and I was thankful due to among other things my lack of head protection. Just then we were stopped again, and this time the three of us with about a dozen other men were lead to the right once more while the rest of the group continued on ahead. I began to wonder if we were lost in our own damn trench system when suddenly we stopped again in front of a large dugout. As we formed into attention as best we could, given the restricted space, our Unteroffizer went in and I could hear him report loudly once inside. He must have made a hasty report because no sooner had he entered than he emerged again and marched right passed us without saying a word. I was really confused, since this wasn't our trench from what I could remember of it. Had we been reassigned? Suddenly a fear gripped me; what if we were being fed into a new unit? What if we never saw Pangloss again? Would they put us into the firing line without giving us our promised leave? My heart began to race as my mind swooned with the possibilities.

The panic inside of me was rising rapidly now, and I felt myself glancing around wildly for someone or something to comfort me. Lars was fidgeting rather spastically next to me, and Rolf was making little simpering noises as he buttoned and then unbuttoned the top button of his tunic. Where we going mad? No one else around us seemed to notice us. Where we going mad?? I was seriously starting to contemplate making a break for it, and was about to tug on Lars' sleeve to get his attention when suddenly a roar of voices and laughter burst forth from the dugout before us, followed by the emergence of an NCO. Instinctively we all snapped to, though at the moment I felt like I was about to faint. He came stepping out with his head over his shoulder, as if he was looking back to say one last thing, and in the process stumbled slightly as he came up level to us. Suddenly my spinal fluid stiffened again; it was Pangloss! Instantly my terror melted away and my heartrate began to slow, and I could hear the sigh that hissed through Lars' teeth next to me that told me that he was feeling the same way. "Attention! For the benefit of the new faces here, of which there are many, I am Sergeant Pangloss. For those of you who already know me, I am still Sergeant Pangloss." At this, there was a roar of laughter from within the dugout, followed by the emergence of another Sergeant who came stumbling up the stairs with a tin cup in one hand and a kitten in the other. Was I going mad? At this Pangloss took the cup from the other Sergeant and took a long drink, and then took the kitten from him as he handed back the cup. "Attention men! This is our new, top-secret war winning weapon. It is so secret that not even Crown Prince Rupprecht knows of its development! Once unleashed, the French won't know what hit them—we'll just have to walk into Paris and piss in the Seine and then the war will be over. Men! Behold…this is Minka." At that, he held the little kitten aloft, which to its credit it seemed to enjoy, and at that another roar of laughter came from within the dugout. Was I going mad?

Just as I was about to rub my eyes and see if all that I had just witnessed would still be there once my vision cleared the scene before us began to shift. The kitten was returned to the dugout and several more NCOs emerged in more or less a similar state of affairs, but despite the drunkenness order quickly came to the situation. Pangloss walked over to us three and stopped in front of me, adjusting his crumpled feldmutze and crooked collar before beginning to speak. When he did so, he spoke in a hushed tone, as if to keep that he knew us a secret from the rest. "You sons-of-bitches made it, I can't believe it. Well, your good Sergeant is true to his word. I have your medals and accompanying paperwork in my desk, as well as the signed documents that allow all three of you a week's leave. Keep the leave to yourselves! Not everyone was treated so generously. In a few moments, we will be marching back to our trench, which you will be pleasantly surprised to find still just as you left it, and will be retrieving your belongings before being mustered out for your leave. Any questions?"

"Yes, Sergeant." Lars had perhaps too cocky of a tone to his voice, but Pangloss was drunk and didn't seem to notice. "We haven't been issued any helmets and yet we are about to be headed up to the front line. I believe we all lost ours when we were hurt, too. So what's to be done? I don't need to get shot in the head just as I'm about to go on leave." Pangloss let out a chuckle and slapped Lars on the shoulder. "Smart boy! But not to worry, the German army always provides." At that, he walked away (stumbling a bit I must add) to rejoin the rest of his soused group. I could see that they were all packing up and getting ready to move off, and several of them where struggling to fold up a small table and to close a small wooden field desk (another was struggling to get his pistol back in its holster, to which I was watching intensely, while still another was putting the kitten in a bread bag that was slung around his neck). Once the field desk was closed the same two Sergeants carried a rather large wooden crate over to the side of the road and kicked the already-loosened lid off before walking away. At that, the command was given to 'fall in,' to which we all formed a line of files facing back from whence we came and then began to move out. As we began to march foreword I could see that our route brought us past the open crate in the road, and as each man passed he stooped down and grabbed a helmet as he did so. The German army always provides…this was clearly a crate of field pickings, because the helmet I grabbed was muddy and dented and was missing the chin strap. Furthermore it was at least a size too big if not more, and as a result it moved all over my head as we turned out and began to head down a twisting and narrow communication trench that apparently lead to our own front line. As I looked up at Lars (who was in front of me) I gasped to myself: The helmet he grabbed had a large and rather jagged-looking hole in the back of it. I shuddered as I pictured what the original owner's head must have looked like when that hole was acquired, and decided at that moment not to point it out to Lars lest he hadn't noticed it when he put it on—or the condition of the interior of the helmet for that matter.

It was all coming back to me now…it wasn't long before we were all back in familiar territory. As amazing as it may seem one can always recognize his own section of trench, and when finally we made another sharp right (which as a group was a slow and careful process, made more complicated by our semi-convalescent and the NCO's semi-drunken state) we were suddenly back home—in fact we were back to the stretch of trench that we were in for our last fateful breakfast that 'construction duties' morning. As we all fell into line several of the NCO's staggered on ahead, while for us Pangloss addressed us as we stood in line. "Men, you have all been briefed at this point, and all have been given varying instructions. See to those instructions now! I will remain here for 30 minutes but then must depart for headquarters." At this, he shot us a knowing glance as he dismissed the group, and at that everyone spread out to go and seek their fortunes. I couldn't believe we were back here, it looked as if nothing had changed since we left that morning! Was there still a war on? And why was it so quiet? How bizarre it all was, the entire experience we just had. I was just about to ask my companions their thoughts when Rolf came slinking around from behind me to tap Lars on the shoulder. As Lars turned around to face him a thin little smile began to creep out across Rolf's lips. "Nice hole," was all Rolf said, and then he walked off down the trench to presumably grab his gear. And with that about two hours-worth of nervous laughter burst out of me while Lars reddened and flew into a tantrum. "What did he say? Hey! What did you say? Goddammit Kurt what did he say to me?" All I could do was laugh and point to his helmet, to which he responded by pulling it off his head and looking at it seemingly for the first time. "Oh Goddammit Kurt! Someone got their fucking head blown to pieces in this thing!" He then reached back and pitched it with all his might over the parapet toward the French lines, to which much to our sudden horror a rifle shot came flying back overhead in response. Everyone around us sort of ducked or winced, but Lars and I threw ourselves onto the trench floor and stayed there frozen for what seemed like an eternity. I don't know what came over me— certainly I have been shot at before, and furthermore the shot that passed us was harmless, but just the same the sudden appearance of gunfire seemed to knock the wind out of me. I glanced over at Lars who I found to be staring wild-eyed back at me, but before either of us could speak another round went off, this time seemingly from our own lines, and was followed directly by a small cheer of men.

Thankfully no one seemed to notice us on the floor of the trench which would have drawn scorn from our comrades. As we struggled back to our feet Lars noticed me wincing a bit and lent me a hand, which was a welcome gesture from him. "Are you okay? How's the knee?"

Such kind words from one who was just cursing and raging moments before. "I'm alright. That was the first time I've bent it like that since we've been back and it caught me off guard is all. Let's go see why everyone was cheering." To be honest my knee had been bothering me the entire march back to our trench, and me falling on it just now was almost excruciating. I found myself now suddenly hoping to not have to run any time soon. As we rose and dusted ourselves off we started for where we thought the shot rang out from our lines. After passing through a few traverses, we came upon an open area in front of a dugout with a group of men crowded around. Scanning the group I found mostly new faces, though the stature of one in particular stood out and made me suspect that an old nemesis was still with us.

"Hey, would you look at this, if it isn't Hansel and Gretel returning from playing in the forest. Were you two caught and locked in a cage by a witch? How did you manage to escape?"

Yep, it was Jürgen, who immediately disappointed me by not getting himself killed in our absence. "Fuck you, Jürgen." Lars shot him an almost homicidal look, and either due to the fire in his eyes or the scars all over his face Jürgen immediately backed down. In fact, he almost backed up, too. I chose to step between them rather than let whatever was going to happen play out any further. "What's going on here, Jürgen? Did that shot come from over here?" Jürgen looked at me with a slight look of apprehension, and then just pointed to the man at the center of the group of soldiers. A sniper! I had only heard from rumor that the German army was bringing professional snipers into the trenches, but up until now I hadn't actually seen one. There he was; he was tall and slender, with an almost fabulous mustache that curled up on either end, and was of swarthy complexion. He was an older man, too, older even than many of the junior officers that I had seen. He had a special helmet on or rather, a special armor plate attached to the front of his helmet—a stirnpanzer, and was wearing a canvas vest over his uniform that was a mottled brown, green, and yellow color. The trench had been modified where he was set up as well by some sort of armor plate being installed at the ground level, with earth and sandbags piled around it to both offer protection and to mask its location from the French. It looked to have a little door in the center that covered a porthole, which I assumed is where he would fire from rather than expose himself by firing over the top. What a clever setup! I then noticed that there were chalk marks on the wall of the armor plate, which told me that this fellow had been busy. "His name is Dieter. Rumor has it that the German army called him out of retirement on account of his shooting skills. I also heard that he was a professional hunter from the German-African colonies who wanted to hunt for more dangerous game here in France. Then again, I also heard that he was a Hohenzollern and that he is reporting every kill directly to the Kaiser…"

At this, I shot Jürgen a glance as if to say 'enough,' to which he only replied with a wry smile. Then I noticed it—his rifle. His sniper's rifle. It was standing up at the moment, rested on a sandbag and leaning against the right side of the armor plate. What a fantastic looking piece of equipment it was. It looked very similar to the Geweher 98 that we had all been issued, but it had a long, black telescope mounted on the top of it, and the wooden stock seems to have been shortened under the barrel. Plus it looked like the bolt handle had been modified so that it turned down, which is something I wished all of our rifles had since the straight bolt handles that regular issue rifles had were awkward to cycle when firing quickly. He also had some sort of cloth wrapped around the middle of the stock, and a leather pad affixed to the butt where it rested against the shooter's shoulder. I bet that pad made it possible to shoot that rifle all day without getting a sore shoulder. I bet that's how he racked up so many chalk marks, by not having a sore shoulder. I then suddenly found myself wondering what it would be like to look through the telescope at the Frenchmen opposite us. How far away could you see through it? Could you see an individual's face before you shot him? Could you see him grimace when he was hit? Was it easier or was it harder to kill someone when you picked them out individually and marked them for death? I would probably make a horrible sniper, since I'd probably think too much. Plus I wasn't a very good shot.

"Come on, Kurt, let's go get our gear. Remember, Pangloss only gave us a half an hour." Lars' voice of reason suddenly ended my sniper rifle daydream, and he was right, too. We had better get a move on. It wasn't far to get to our old dugout, but the question was, would our gear still be there once we reached it? We had after all been in the field hospital for a couple weeks, and unless someone had specifically stepped in and vouchsafed for our gear it was liable to be long gone. Upon reaching our station, we were able to breathe yet another sigh of relief—both Lars and I found our footlockers to be sealed with jute and tagged with a cardboard tag that read 'headquarters hold.' I knew that Pangloss must have been the one to look out for us, especially since it was he who visited us in the hospital. We both broke off to hurriedly pack our sea bags for our week's leave. I grabbed all the undergarments I had plus some clean socks, my clean change of field uniform, my wallet and all of the papiermarks I had managed to set aside, my feldmutze, and finally, my mother's old handkerchief that was wrapped around something that had been on my mind lately. I then grabbed my cleanest dirty uniform to change into and began to disrobe. In doing so, something small began to whisper in my ear, a little voice that told me to turn around. I couldn't at first understand why, but I suddenly found myself stopping and despite my near nudity first glancing over my shoulder and then finally turning around to see Lars standing there undressed across the room. Funny thing is, when I finally looked at him I found him to be staring at me, and when our gazes met we were both temporarily stunned and not a little embarrassed. He was first to speak. "I guess I was just curious to see if anything was missing after what happened to us. You know, to see if you had any holes in you. Now that I can see it your knee doesn't look as bad as I had figured it would."

I kind of cocked my head at him and laughed a little. "You were expecting something to be blown off? Well I'm glad that your fears can now be laid to rest. Now that you mention it, you don't look too terrible yourself, your face seems to have played the hero by taking the whole hit for you." At that, Lars and I both burst out into laughter, and were at that moment dangerously close to being the old chums that we were before we got wounded. However we had to cut it short and get dressed, as we surely didn't have much time to get back to Pangloss. I threw on my uniform, decided on second thought to slip my mother's handkerchief into my bag for now, threw on my boots and my feldmutze, and then threw my bag over my shoulder and was off. Lars was right behind me, and we beat it back to the entrance to our trenchline where Pangloss said he'd be waiting. He was there all right, tapping his trench watch and raising an eyebrow at us when we arrived. Rolf was there too, sitting cross-legged on his sea bag and smiling up at us. "You two are late. If it wasn't for my good graces, you two wouldn't be going anywhere. Now put your bags down and fall in in front of me. That means you too Rolf."

We instantly did as we were told, all forming a quick little line in front of him while he carefully opened a large paper envelope that he had taken from the inside of his tunic. Out from the envelope came three small cardboard boxes that when opened revealed dark colored medals that we instantly recognized to be Iron Crosses, Second Class. He then approached us three, individually pinning our badges to our tunics and shaking our hands directly afterwards. After he was done, he handed us each a sealed envelope that contained both our certificate of wounding with its thanks from the Kaiser and our signed leave paperwork. He then smiled at us three, folded the old envelope up and slid it into his back pocket, and then bade us to pick up our bags and follow after him. With that, we were off. "An Iron Cross...can you believe it Kurt? An *Iron Cross*! We are going to get laid for these, mark my words..." Lars' voice trailed off as he undoubtedly began to visualize himself behind a barmaid, his Iron Cross gleaming majestically in the greasy candlelight as it rested on the careworn bedside table of her boudoir. I for one was feeling rather nonplussed, and oddly enough found myself at that very moment wondering what ever had happened to Pangloss' little friend Minka as we followed him through the endless maze of communication trenches that eventually lead us back to green grass and singing birds.

# Chapter Eleven
# Die Franzosen

So finally the mystery has been solved: They've simply been moved. Or more specifically, due to a perceived increase in pressure at another sector of the front which seemed to herald a German build-up and possible offensive they've been sent there as a defensive measure. The reason why the heavy guns that we thought had pulverized the boches during that bizarre bombardment have not been fired since is because they are gone. Whether or not the bombardment they unleashed on the German rear-areas was intended to be followed up by some sort of offensive action is a moot question at this point I suppose, yet it still crosses my mind. I have a feeling that whomever it was that decided to build up the heavies behind our lines and then pound the boches with them was expecting different results, and more importantly had convinced his superiors of different results, and so therefore when the outcome was what it was he had his toy guns taken away. So now we sit, and wait, and endure the increased traffic in munitions between their lines and ours. And while the strafing flights have been reduced dramatically which has been a blessing, the flights seem to have been replaced with the work of a rather skilled sniper. I now wouldn't dare peek my head up over a parapet, anywhere, and bid my men strictly to do the same. Of course he has still gotten some—especially those who venture to think that they can play at his game—and furthermore the threat that he generates has been all out of proportion to the actual casualties he inflicts. His mere presence makes us all uneasy, and now all the men go about stooped so low that a simple greeting is rendered ridiculous by their postures. At least you can usually hear an aero-plane coming, or even the whine of a trench mortar bomb (though you haven't much time to seek shelter if you do), but a sniper was truly sudden death. Just this morning a young and still clean-shaven poilu decided to try and end this business all by himself—

and paid an instant and heavy toll for his heroics. Before I had even the chance to discover who was doing the shooting, our young hero lay sprawled across the floor of the trench with his jaw shot away and portion of his skull rent open by a Mauser bullet. At the moment I discovered his body I had half a mind to make an example out of him, and contemplated parading all the new faces past him in order that they might catch a glimpse of his thoughts, but instead I just settled on putting in for a request for either a sniper to be sent to our section as a countermeasure or in the very least a good pair of field glasses be sent up in order that I may discover the location of *their* sniper. But since neither have been forthcoming as of yet we sit, and we wait, and we endure this protracted riposte to our late artillery demonstration.

Which is really the frustrating part. I almost long to do something, *anything*, anything other than hunker down and endure. I'm not saying that I necessarily wish to attack the lines opposite of ours, but I almost wouldn't mind them attacking us in some sort of fashion. At least if they did, we'd be sure to kill scores of them in the process. I'm afraid that it's been so long since some of these men have fired their rifles that when called upon to do so they might not even remember *how*. At this point, I'd even settle for manual labor; improving our stretch of front line would be welcome, as would digging a few saps out into no-man's land for listening or even bomb-tossing. Anything to occupy my men's time, and honestly mine as well. For I fear that the men around me are starting to lose their will to combat, their fighting edge, and I'm starting to even question myself. Apathy, alcoholism, and chronic masturbation plague this section of the line, while seemingly not even the stalking threat of death or dismemberment is enough to make more of an impression on the men other than to alter their postures when walking about. Honestly, and I'm almost ashamed to think it, I wouldn't be surprised to find out that some of this new German sniper's kills have actually been purposeful woundings with the hopes for a ticket home, or even suicides. How easy it would be to get one's self shot and into an ambulance…then again, your head is the first thing to be seen over the parapet…

What really needs to happen, what needs to be done is a rotation for the men up here, myself included. I've heard that the British have a very rigid system in place for their front-line soldiers, whereby they serve given stints of time in the foreword trench and then are rotated through the support trenches and then given a short leave before returning to the front. Now admittedly this sounds like a bit of fantasy, but I happen to know that their troops are rotated, at least on the most active fronts. I get the feeling that the Germans have some system in place as well though I cannot profess as to the specifics. Yet here we sit, day after day, week after week, only being topped off with new men to fill in the gaps left by the morning hate and the daily wastage. If this section could just be given some time off, some time to get cleaned up, well fed, drunk, laid, etc., the men would be completely restored and back up to fighting strength. Then again, if the average man here was given a week to run amok amongst the cafes and bedrooms of Paris he might well never be seen again when it was time to come put his horizon blue back on and head back up to the front. That's the fear that the men that run this show have at any rate, that if the average poilu was given any time away from the front that he would never come back. Better to keep us here in this stinking mud hole than risk the effects of us feeling happy for a few days. Happy. That's a word that has come to mean so many things, both tangible and abstract, since my life was transformed into the reality that I live now from what it once was before this all happened. Now happy can mean anything; Happy because I lived today (though not always), because I got drunk today (though not always), because I ate hot food today (though not always), because I shit today (though not always). Every little thing that has the potential to bring joy has also the potential to bring sorrow. And so happy is fleeting, and has different meanings depending on the day.

Right now things are calm, which admittedly is enough to make me happy for the moment. I have the urge for a drink but I've already had quite a bit of wine so far today and have a headache, which could be from the wine. Or yesterday's wine. It's been a long time since I've cleaned my pistol and so I could do that, but then again, it's also been a long time since it was fired and so it's probably not that dirty. *C'est la vie.* I decide to go for a walk through the trench line ostensibly to inspect my men, and I mostly find them hard at work on their little trinkets. Tiny little baubles made from a driving band or a shell casing, or even a shell splinter. They look like dwarves sometimes, bent over their little treasures with files and hammers and whatever else they can find for tools. It's funny, the men put so much time and effort into these little things that their value gets blown all out of proportion compared to their equipment of real import. I've encountered many a poilu that hadn't any eating utensils or a plate, or who had misplaced his rifle cleaning kit, but that knew right away where his tiny little inkwell was that he's been working on for a month. Comical really, that this unnatural war could transform us into dwarves and gypsies, making and hawking little trinkets out of bits of trash. I wonder if any of them consider being toymakers after the war but then again, given the overwhelming sense of apathy that pervades here I would imagine that no one is thinking too much about life after this *afternoon*, let alone the war. My inspection complete, the thought hits me to maybe have that drink after all. As I pour some pinard into my battered tin cup and sit down on an empty bomb crate my mind wanders onto nothing in particular. Slowly I begin to make out the tiny little hammers of my men as they bang away at their projects, and I subconsciously begin to pretend that I'm a little German dwarf that lives under a mountain, while at the same time I'm mindful to keep my head down from the German sniper across the way.

# Chapter Twelve
# Les Allemands

Metz. Metz Germany. *That* Metz Germany, the one that was still France before our father's war shifted the German frontier from the Rhine to the Moselle. *That* Metz was apparently as far as our week's pass from Pangloss would take us. He had mentioned that he couldn't guarantee us a trip home but this was a disappointingly far cry from it. As we three stepped down from our train car and onto the pavement I had to forcibly stifle my disappointment at the surroundings. I had heard that the city was half destroyed before it surrendered to our army back in '70, but from the looks of things it had still very much been in the process of being rebuilt when our current war broke out. Everything looked gray and sullen, including the people, and I felt a chill run up my spine when I contemplated how much German soldiers must be hated in this place. I had heard stories about how much the French citizens that lived here resented becoming Germans by force, and now I could see it written all over the faces of those who happened to meet our gaze as we stepped down from the platform and onto the plaza that surrounded the station. "Hey Kurt, come on, let's find a lavatory so that we can get cleaned up, and so that we can make sure our medals look good." Lars was eyeing our surroundings like a locust bent on delivering a plague. "Plus I'm sure that you'd like to splash your face and drag a comb through your hair before we set out to see the sights." At the word 'sights,' he winked at me and tugged a little at the groin of his uniform trousers, which I found to be both vulgar and inexplicably intriguing. Before we could even set out, however, a voice boomed from behind us and forced us back into the moment. "You three, come this way. You will show me your leave papers now!" A towering figure of a Feldgendarmerie Sergeant glowered over us as we all three sheepishly produced our envelopes that contained our leave papers. After he carefully inspected each one, he produced a small inkstamp from a leather bag that he had slung around his shoulder, and then checked his large pocket watch before stamping each one with today's date and the current time. "You three have exactly seven days from this moment to be back here, though the trains do not always run on the hour and so I recommend that you familiarize yourselves with their schedule. Be on your guard! Many of the faces you will meet will not be friendly, mind your business wherever you go. You three are German citizens in a German territory, yet many of the city's inhabitants are war refugees from various places and furthermore, due to the city's French past it is hard for us to know who belongs here and who does not. Don't let yourselves be taken for fools or mix with bad company! Finally, I am here to warn you: I expect you three to conduct yourselves in accordance to the law and the laws of decency. Us Feldgendarmerie are everywhere in the city, see to it that you don't do something to land yourself in a holding cell for the duration of your leave." At that, he patted Lars on the shoulder (probably because due to his profession he could already spot which one of us was trouble) and then turned to walk away.

"Wait, sir, just one moment. Can you at least provide us with some direction? None of us have ever been to Metz before."

He stopped and smiled at me. "What kind of direction do you want, young man? As a man of the law…"

He purposely let his voice trail off as he patted the truncheon that hung from his belt. "Oh, sir, nothing like that. We just would like to know where we can get something to eat, and perhaps to drink. Where do soldiers generally go here?"

He smiled at me again, and twisted the end of his iron-gray mustache as if he was suddenly deep in thought. "Place Saint-Louis. Yes, that's it. It is an open space where people gather, and around it there are many pubs and cafes where you three can relax. I know the soldiers go there often. Just head that way about a kilometer or so and you will run into it. Now if you'll excuse me I must take my leave." At 'that way', he motioned down the street behind us with his hand, and once he excused himself he turned and walked back up the stairs of the train platform and then disappeared into the crowd. "What a lucky break! Those chained dogs are usually bastards, thank God that we ran into one that let us off like he did."

Lars cracked his knuckles as he began to look around us again, and had a look on his face like he had just gotten away with something. "Lavatory?" I turned to our friend Rolf who had been silent up to this point and laughed.

"Yes, right! Lars, you had wanted to find a place to clean up." Soon the three of us started off down the street toward this Saint-Louis place and before we had gone very far came upon a pissoir that was next to a public fountain. This meagre facility would suit our needs for the moment, and so all three of us ducked in to take care of our various businesses.

There was a large, dirty mirror someone had nailed to the back wall of the facility, and I set my bag down in front of it in order to look myself over and to adjust things. After fixing my collar and brushing back my greasy hair, I made sure that my Iron Cross was straight and secure. Then a little voice reminded me about my mother's handkerchief that I had thrown in my bag at the last minute. Pausing, I reached down into my bag and retrieved it, and gazed at it for a few minutes in my hand before opening it and unwrapping my father's old jagdnicker knife. I paused once more before undoing the leather clasp of the makeshift sheath and sliding it up and around my heavy leather uniform belt. I then looked at myself again in the mirror; the knife seemed so small to me as it hung at my side, it almost appeared to be a toy. Funny, it always seemed so big when I was a boy. I carefully folded my mother's handkerchief back up and placed it back in my bag and then headed back out to see where my companions were. "You're wearing your knife? Wow, thanks a lot. I figured it would be easy to get laid with our medals but now the girls are all going to go for the mountain man." Lars punched me in the shoulder and then went to knock my feldmutze off, but I ducked out of the way and then straightened back up and adjusted my medal. Lars seemed to get my demeanor and left me alone, instead choosing to make a face at Rolf who was at the moment staring at his reflection in the fountain. "I don't like that everything around here still has Frenchy names. This is Germany now after all, isn't it? Take this Saint-Louis place that we're headed to. I don't like the sound of it, it should have a German name. And I don't like the idea of the city being full of cloak-and-dagger Frenchmen either…" Lars' voice trailed off as he looked around with a suspicious look on his face. "Don't be ridiculous. There's a war on, remember? There are shady characters everywhere in every big city, even Munich. Now come on, I could use a beer." We three picked up our bags and continued down the street, passing dirty little shops with hardly anything in their windows and shabby little cafes with no one sitting in them. This was a far cry from how things looked in my hometown when I marched through with my new regiment toward the train station that would take me to the frontier and eventually to France. Back then people everywhere were laughing and singing and waving little flags—a young girl with pretty blond braids even walked right up to me and kissed me on the cheek as I marched past. Everything was so colorful and gay—what happened? Wasn't Germany winning the war? After all, we are fighting the French in France, not the other way around. Where were all the happy people? I was able to justify my surroundings by simply chalking it up to us being in Metz, which was to us like still being back in France. Yet still I found the eerie silence and empty streets unsettling, and even perhaps foreboding in a way. Were things really not going that well in the war after all? Were the three of us really safe here by ourselves? I suddenly found myself gripped with a similar panic to the one that overtook me when we first ventured back into the trenches after our convalescence in the field hospital. What was wrong with me? My pulse quickened as I looked over at Lars. "Hey, are you okay?" Lars was squinting his eyes up the street to see if he could catch a street name or anything else that might help tell us where we are.

"No, I'm not okay. I want a beer and some soft company, and I'm getting tired of carrying this bag."

At that, Rolf chimed in with "Yeah, a beer," to which I couldn't help but laugh at. Okay, I'm the only one that's not okay. Gathering myself up I tried to effect a nonchalant air. "Yeah, this Saint-Louis place had better be close because I am getting pretty curious to see what kind of beer will be available. What do you think Lars? Will it be Lager or Pilsner?" I looked at Lars with the best forced smirk that I could muster, but at the moment he was leaning forward and cocking his head.

"Wait! Be quiet. Do you hear that?" Once our hobnailed boots were still on the cobblestones I heard it too; a faint strain of music and of people talking and laughing. We must be close! All three of us looked at each other and simultaneously tossed our bags up onto our shoulders as if we were about to dash up scaling ladders and hurl ourselves at the enemy.

Place Saint-Louis was a large open space surrounded by buildings on all sides, mostly older residential buildings with shops, pubs, and cafes on the ground floor. It was large, several blocks long by at least one wide, and was full of people coming and going. There were many other German soldiers mixed into the crowd (which was oddly disappointing), as well as everyday people either out for a walk, sitting down for a meal or a drink, or plying the crowded plaza with their trades-be them legitimate or not. Music wafted through the air over the din and clatter, which drew my attention to a small band playing in the center of the square that was for the moment roughly handing a Chopin waltz. The combined odors of food and tobacco, perfume and garbage, and beer and urine alternately meandered through the air and felt both enticing and nauseating as we were drawn into this strange oasis within this otherwise unwelcoming city. "This must be it! Let's go grab a table by a pub and get a few beers and then see where the day takes us."

Lars was fairly straining at the leash by now. "Okay, that sounds like a great idea, though you still never answered me as to whether you think they are going to have pilsners of lagers…" Lars moved off before I could really even finish my sentence and before I knew it Rolf and I were doing everything we could to just keep up with him. Before us out of the crowd loomed a large, noisy pub that had its wall of wooden doors swung open to reveal a gaggle of German soldiers milling about with bierkrugs in their hands. It was standing room only, but the crowd seemed to be falling back before us somehow as we nosed up to the bar and motioned for the barkeep's attention.

Lars had three beers ordered for us in no time (I guess I'd *still* have to wait to find out whether they served pilsners or lagers) and even bought the first round. Bierkrugs in hand we three wormed our way back out into the fresh air and luckily happened to find a tottery old cafe table that was unoccupied for the moment. It felt great to finally lay my heavy sea bag down, and it felt even better to finally pour some beer down my throat (it was a lager). The three of us stood there for what seemed like a long time, each of us alternately drinking from our bierkrugs and then looking around at our strange surroundings. Each time Rolf took a drink he'd let the foam rest on his upper lip afterwards, which gave him the appearance of a child who'd been given a saucer of buttermilk. He'd then wipe the foam away with his shirtsleeve and repeat the process with the same childish gleam in his eye. I suspected that he hadn't drank many beers up to this point in his life and resolved myself to keep an eye on him lest he overdo it and become one more heavy thing for me to carry. After a particularly satisfying pull on my beer, I turned to Lars and was about to ask him how he felt when we were suddenly approached for the first time since arriving here.

"Good afternoon, comrades, welcome to our little slice of France! Say, you three came from the front, right? Did we win yet?" This frontschwein had clearly been in the bottle all afternoon, and I had already made my mind up to tell him to bugger off when he persisted in his conversation.

"Hey, wow, Iron Crosses huh? You three have seen some shit then right? There's a couple guys here from my unit, we're from Baden, and one of them has an Iron Cross…"

This was *not* the attention that we had hoped these medals would garner. I could tell that Lars was about to make a terse statement to our new associate when he again beat him to it. "I'm Volker, I'm drunk, and I don't care about this war any more. I'm only on leave because most of the men in my section were all killed at once, and so high command thought it best to give us few survivors a break before feeding us back into the grinder." I really didn't give a shit about this guy's story, but I could tell that Rolf was intrigued.

"We got blown up. All of us, blown up." All three of us turned and stared at Rolf after he was done. Volker because he was drunk and surprised to hear what Rolf had said, and Lars and I because we were surprised to hear Rolf say more than three syllables at one time. "Blown up huh? Wow. How'd that feel?" He laughed and then turned to me and put his hand on the table in front of me, either to hold himself up or to try and give the impression that he had something important to say. "And what about you? Say, that's a *nice knife*. You must be from the Black Forest to wear a hunting knife like that. Where'd you get it?"…

It had been a rather cold morning, and my mother had insisted that I put on my woolen jacket and fur-lined hat before heading out. It was late fall, which was when the children in my village traditionally were sent by their parents into the woods to gather nuts for the upcoming winter. My sister was still really too small to be of any real help and so my mother had her stay home, ostensibly to help her with house chores. Off I went, satchel in hand, knowing full well that I needn't return until it was brimming with walnuts, hazelnuts, and beechnuts; all of which I was taught at a young age to recognize and how to harvest. Nutting was a traditional pastime that helped stock up the pantry for the long winter months ahead, though I must admit that all I really cared about was that it meant that if I found enough walnuts my mother would bake walnut bread which I was particularly fond of. I was fond of nutting, too. It gave me a chance to stalk the woods alone like I was game hunting, even if it were only for such innocuous game as walnuts. I always nutted alone, which looking back was I guess a bit odd since most of the other children in my village went out nutting in little groups together. It was safer that way, I guess, being in a group. But I never seemed to belong to a group as a child and so I had no group to go out in even if I wanted to. Besides, I felt safer in the woods than I did anywhere else. Anyway. Unfortunately for me the woods close to home seemed to have been rather worked over by the time I reached them that day, which meant that I'd be wandering farther afield than I had initially hoped. I shrugged it off, figuring that my longer absence from home would just give my mother more time to herself since my father had left for business earlier that morning.

After a few hours' work my bag had begun to get heavy, as did my arms from all the lifting and tree shaking. Judging by how low the sun was in the sky I had figured that it was about time to head back home anyway and besides, I was starting to catch a chill. The woods that I had been working in were damp and in the process of my day's efforts I had become rather sodden, which now caused my thoughts to drift from walnuts to dry clothes and a warm fire. Still, I told myself as I started back for home to at least keep my eyes peeled for any missed pickings on the way back as admittedly I could have fit more nuts into my bag had I wanted to. Before long, I was trudging up the road that lead out of town and as I approached our house I made the snap decision to go around back and enter through the kitchen door. My boots were muddy, as was my satchel, and I knew that my mother had probably spent the day cleaning and would therefore be rather sensitive to me introducing a mess to our front parlor. As I walked up the four steps that led to the landing and opened the door to enter the kitchen it struck me as odd that the house was so dark, given that the sun had just about set on my journey home. I set my satchel down by the table and used the feeble light streaming in from the open door to grab a lucifer match from the safe on the wall to light the lantern on the table. As I pulled off my coat and sat down to unlace my boots I caught a strange muffled noise that seemed to come from the other side of the house. After I took off my boots, I grabbed the lantern and set out to investigate the noise and to find where my family was.

Our house was small and of typical rural design, meaning that it didn't take long to find that no one was on the ground floor in any of the rooms. I paused to consider lighting the fireplace in the parlor but just as I did I caught another strain of that same muffled noise coming from the upstairs of our house. I figured that the fire could wait, and headed for the staircase. The upstairs of the house was dark, save for a shaft of muted, flickering candlelight that streamed feebly from the cracked door to my parent's bedroom. As I crept slowly across the wooden floor, careful to avoid the loose boards that I knew squeaked when stepped upon, the noise I had heard downstairs was repeated and this time I heard it more clearly due to my proximity. I froze. I could almost make out what sounded like my father breathing heavily and making little throat noises, and there were sounds of sniffling and what seemed like choking mixed in at random intervals. My first instinct was to turn around and go back downstairs, yet the mixture of curiosity and concern inside of me wouldn't allow it. I pressed on. I set the lantern carefully down on the small table in the hallway before reaching up slowly to push open my parent's bedroom door.

As my eyes adjusted to the eerie candlelight I first made out the figure of my father. He was standing toward the center of the room, facing mostly away from the door, with one hand resting on something in front of him and the other holding an object that I couldn't quite make out in the dark. He seemed unsteady on his feet and to be rocking slightly, which I assumed must have meant that he had taken to drink at some point in the morning or afternoon. I took two small, careful steps into the room and as my eyes further adjusted to the light I discovered the shape of my mother in the flickering shadows. There she was, on her knees before my father. Her blouse was torn open to reveal her disarranged brassiere and heaving bosom; a stream of blood ran down her neck and over the tops of her breasts. Nausea swept over me, and I felt warm and faint. I could hear the pulse of my blood in my ears and feel the sweat beading on my brow. I was embarrassed, no, I was *mortified* at seeing my mother's nakedness. Yet my eyes were fixated on the blood running down her breasts. I felt myself being drawn toward them, the stream of blood growing into a torrent in my mind as I gazed at it pooling grotesquely between them. I couldn't feel my feet on the floor. I could taste the soot from the burning tallow candle in the air. I could smell the wet woods on my damp clothing. Suddenly a reflection of light caught my eye and shook me back into consciousness. I now saw what my father was holding; he held his little jagdnicker in his hand and had it pressed against my mother's face, his other hand holding a clump of her hair as he forced her head before him. I could tell from behind that the cod piece of his lederhosen was unbuttoned by the way it hung down between his legs and swayed back and forth as he moved my mother's head with his hand.

In between thrusts, I was able to glimpse the tears running down my mother's face and could tell that she was struggling to breathe. Suddenly my mother choked and pulled away from him, gasping and coughing as she did so. He let out a growl as he yanked my mother's head back by her hair and pressed the jagdnicker to her throat. She gurgled out a feeble "*bitte*" before sobbing pitifully, her upward gaze dropping from him while her strength seemed to ebb away.

And that is when she saw me.

I don't remember crossing the floor I don't remember actually being hit I don't remember hitting back I don't remember falling down I don't remember getting up I don't remember taking the knife I don't remember using the knife I don't remember crying out I don't remember losing my footing I don't remember the constable's name. I don't remember the doctor's name. I don't remember the coroner's name. I don't remember the pallbearer's names.

I remember my mother handing me her handkerchief as I climbed into the wagon that took me to the train in the next town which took me to another town which had the reform school in it that I was to spend the next five years in before the war broke out and I found myself here.

"It's a family heirloom."

"It's a family heirloom." I could tell from the blank looks on my companion's faces that they must have not heard me the first time.

In fact, they still seemed not to hear. "I said, it's a fam…"

"Okay Kurt, that's enough. That's quite enough. What's wrong with you? C'mon, here, I'll give a Mark to Rolf so that he can go run along and get you a new beer. You don't mind Rolf, right?" I turned my head and furrowed my brow at Lars as if to ask him if HE was okay but instead just ended up watching Rolf scamper away through the crowd with a Papiermark in his hand to apparently go and buy me a new beer.

"Man, I figured you guys had seen some shit, but I didn't think that *this* guy was going to be the fucked up one. Ha! I mean, wow. You know we're not under fire right now, right?" Volker snapped his fingers at me as if I were mesmerized and then kind of motioned with his eyes down toward the ground. "Crazy man!" I had no idea what this Volker was talking about but I was starting to feel as if he was making fun of me somehow and I didn't like it. I was about to straighten him out when Lars reached out and touched my arm in a surprisingly soothing manner; when I looked at him he just motioned with his eyes downwards—which is when I realized that I was only holding the clay handle of my bierkrug. The rest of it was laying shattered on the ground at my feet and its contents were splattered across the toes of my boots. "Just relax Kurt, Rolf will be back soon with a new beer for you. Do you have something in your eye?"

As I stood there feeling a little dumbfounded and rubbing my right hand (and smearing the tears off of my cheek with my uniform sleeve) Lars took it upon himself to try and steer the focus away from me and onto more pressing issues. "Hey Volker, you've been out here for a while now, right? What's the action? What's a good Bavarian boy have to do to meet a nice girl around here?" The compassionate tone was now completely gone from his voice and what replaced it was pure imp. Just as Volker was about to speak Rolf came scampering up and dutifully handed me a new beirkrug full of lager.

"Beer!" is all he said with a smile, and as I took it from him we both turned to listen in on this sure-to-be interesting conversation.

"Women eh? Yeah I bet it's been a long time for you, Frontschwein. Well, I happen to know that there is a laundry not far from here that serves all of these big apartment buildings around us, and that it employs lots of Algerian and Moroccan women from the French colonies. They practically can't say no, hell, they're not even allowed to say no!"

Volker slapped the table in front of him with a flourish and winked absurdly at Lars. "Just think about it, easy pickings. No dinner to buy or drawn-out walks along the Moselle. You just take her by her dark little hand and lead her over to a pile of laundry…" My mind started to reel as Volker talked about raping laundresses. Why would you *have* to *rape* them? What if you met a pretty little Algerian girl and she was impressed by your uniform, or your Iron Cross, or what if she spoke a little German and was impressed by all your war stories? Maybe you two could split a bottle of wine after her washing shift was over at one of these nice little café tables, maybe with a little candle and a little vase of flowers. Maybe you'd make her laugh, maybe she'd seem exotic and alluring to you. Maybe she would share an apartment with some other washer girls who worked a different shift than her and who wouldn't be home at the moment. Maybe she'd invite you to her apartment in her own coy little way, and maybe you'd feign being shy and say yes. Maybe she'd take you home and treat you like a sultan, pleasing you with her seductive lovemaking while her exotic ululations echoed off the walls of her bedchamber…

"I could never fuck a *neger*." Lars spit on the pavement and wrinkled his nose in disgust.

"It would be like laying with a barn animal." Lars' deplorable reply slapped me across the face and snapped me back into the present. I had to clear my throat and adjust my trousers while pretending to think that what Lars had said was somehow funny.

"Ha! Picky picky I see. Well I hate to inform you, but as the saying goes, beggars can't be choosers. All the decent—and many of the indecent—woman around here are spoken for one way or the other. We've been at war now for so long and had so many soldiers file through here that there isn't a girl above 14 who hasn't done her part for the war effort if you get my meaning. Hell, take that coffee shop there behind us. It's run by a tolerably attractive woman whose husband is off somewhere at the front. She's currently pregnant—as is her 16-year-old daughter—and get this! The same plucky German soldier knocked them both up!" I was having a tough time stifling the urge to strangle this Volker character just now, and was struggling to find a way to create a diversion that could change the topic of the conversation. I was about to ask Lars for a cigarette when Volker again beat me to the punch.

"Nope, no decent women around here to be had, unless there is some stash locked away in a cellar somewhere. You'll either have to settle for what you can take or pay for it—and the professionals are currently operating at wartime inflation rates!"

# Chapter Thirteen
# Die Franzosen

So it all started with a bang. Or rather, a rather large explosion of a rather large trench mortar shell in the middle of an otherwise peaceful afternoon. It caught this entire section off guard but thankfully only wounded a few. There wasn't much time to think about it when it happened either, because it wasn't long before many more just like it came flying over to plaster us and drive us down into the recesses of our dugouts and scrapes. It was honestly the heaviest mortar bombardment I'd ever been through, and as it turned out it heralded a new attitude held by the boches opposite of us for this little slice of stagnated front that we call home. In an afternoon, our stretch went from relatively quiet to unpredictably menacing. We started receiving concentrated bombardments at irregular intervals, some of which lifted only to unleash brief Stormtrooper-like assaults where small groups of heavily armed German soldiers rushed out at us to try and gain entry to our trenchlines—almost like a trench raid in broad daylight only with heavy weapons instead of clubs. Also there has been a renewed presence in the air of the German air wing, only now they mostly strafe us with machine guns or drop small bombs from low altitudes. This is all very terrifying and of course has warranted a response from our side of no-man's land. In addition to our ever present 75's who gamely hurl shells toward the Germans at the slightest provocation, we now have some wonderful trench mortars of our own. Our British allies, who now occupy a stretch of the front adjacent to us, have bestowed upon us a battery of Stokes mortars. After showing us how to use them and incorporating our section into their ammo resupply system, we have effectively put them to good use against the lines opposite ours. Now we find ourselves banging away merrily at the boches with our mortars while at the same time absorbing punishment from theirs in kind. When things get too hot, we dive underground for cover and I send up green very lights (also a gift from our British cousins) which brings a torrent of shells from the nearest Schneider batteries behind our lines. Also, as an additional shot in our locker, our aforementioned British cousins have also lent a hand over our lines as well with their plucky little local aero squadron. It is marvelous to see their machines come out and engage the German flying circus that plagues us, or to swoop low over their lines with machine guns blazing.

So I drink a good deal less during the day now, given the renewed spirit of the war that has prevailed around here as of late. Real war can and does visit us here now in the most violent of fashions sometimes multiple times a day, and being blotto certainly does not aid in formulating a response. But the renewed strain, fear, and gore certainly does make me want to reach for a bottle. My nerves are worn raw by the cycle of bombardment, responding bombardment, casualty clearing, and then the inevitable trench rebuilding. Plus the attrition has consumed men at a rate unseen for quite some time—I really don't know who all the men are in my section now and who I exercise nominal control over. I just know that I have to keep my mortar men and machine gunners ready and supplied, and have to try and install confidence in the new recruits as they come out and sometimes become casualties within hours of arrival. And all of that makes me want to have a drink, which now sometimes I cannot have.

This morning I am pleased to be sipping my coffee after eating breakfast, instead of cowering in my hole during a mortar barrage and dreaming of waking up to a cup of coffee instead of a barrage. There was a pretty big show here yesterday that honestly scared the shit out me and made me question whether we could hold in the event of something bigger. Things started out okay—morning hate was on time and lasted about as long as usual. With few casualties to report in my section, we immediately set to firing back our customary response with our British tubes. These are the medium caliber type, and so can hurl a rather large bomb quite easily right down into their trenches despite the distance of no-man's land between us. After running through our customary crate of ammo per gun, I signaled the cease fire and then set about assessing the damage in both men and material.

And that's when the *real* bombardment began.

Out of nowhere a ferocious artillery bombardment descended on our lines and lasted for what seemed like an hour. The initial crash killed many, coming as it did all at once and just as the men were emerging from the shelters that they had hid in from the earlier mortar barrage. Communication was impossible, both within our trench and back to headquarters behind. Had I been able to get off a very light or two it wouldn't have mattered anyway given that the bombardment was throwing up so much smoke and debris. I flung myself down onto the floor of my dugout and pulled my straw stuffed mattress over on top of me. Several other terrified poilus followed me down as well which normally would have been a severe breach of military protocol, but in this instance the rules had gone out the window as the ground around us seethed and boiled like angry surf. Screams and cries were drowned out by the roar of the explosions as the inside of my dugout filled first with dust and then with smoke, and then finally with terrified rats scurrying for cover. Soon breathing became nearly impossible; the air was thick with cordite but what's more, I was beginning to become convinced that we had been gassed and to wonder where my mask was when suddenly the barrage all at once lifted. Run! Run! Run! Everyone out! Bodies frozen in terror had to suddenly lunge into motion and run out toward the very danger they had sought to escape from and to man our battered parapets. I threw my mattress off and saw several men lying stiff on the floor around me, as well as several more standing dazed as they loitered by the doorway and kicked at the frightened rats. With no time to lose, I beat them all out the door (on shaky legs I must admit) and out into whatever was left to defend of our trenchline and our lives.

And not a moment too soon, either. Bullets were already whining overhead and spattering amongst the broken sandbags and twisted wire posts that lay strewn about in the dead space in front of our parapet. We were under attack! Mercifully there was enough breeze to clear the air enough for us to see— which gave us a moment to take in our surroundings and regain our bearings. Many, many in our section had not been lucky enough to find shelter fast enough, if at all. Broken pieces of my men were scattered about and rolled into heaps where they had been pulverized by the violence of the bombardment. Shaking all this off and running toward what was left of the firestep, I leapt over what I thought was a sandbag and in the process kicked an Adrian helmet out of my way to set up a firing position—only to find that the helmet still contained a head of the previous owner that stared back at me as it tumbled down into the shell hole in front of me. There was no time to get sick. Our wire seemed to have been damaged enough that men might get through, and we needed to start laying down fire in order that they didn't. I quickly organized a small machine gun squad out of several riflemen and a machine gun that had been blown from its mount. By means of laying it on a sandbag, it was made passably operational again and was soon laying down fire in long, albeit somewhat inaccurate bursts. Soon fire was spewing forth from up and down the line as my men's training kicked in and they shook off their terror, though in a markedly diminished fashion and made up mostly of rifle fire. My mind went to the Stokes mortars but soon realized that it was already too late to employ them. Glancing out I could now see coal scuttle helmets bobbing up and down toward us, moving in squads and in small rushes from shell hole to shell hole. They'd soon be close to our wire belts, which meant that they'd soon be probing for gaps or creating new ones with cutters. Crash! A potato masher went off in the shell hole in front of our parapet, which wounded a man on the improvised machine gun crew and showered the rest in muddy water. Crash! Another grenade lands near enough to send dirt and detritus over me. Something must be done now if we are to hold this line. I stumbled to my feet and ran down the line with rifle in hand, hoping to install confidence or lend a hand where it was needed. Instead I stumbled upon the disemboweled and legless body of a young Frenchman and his Chauchat, along with a field bag containing six magazines—he fell apart as I lifted the weapon from him but there was no time for revulsion.

From my brief experience with this weapon, I knew to remove the magazine and make sure it's clean before reinserting it and charging the action, lest it jam after the first round. After clearing a bit of its previous owner out of the magazine it seated and the weapon charged, and to my delight fired a flawless burst once I got it up and out over the parapet. Crash! Another grenade goes off to my right, and I see some yards out a boches lean back to throw another. A squeeze of the trigger and he goes down, and as an added bonus his then un-thrown grenade erupts next to his corpse. Hopefully it wounded the others he was with. Suddenly the air around me is alive with the twang and whoosh of bullets! I duck down just as the sweep of the gun passes over the parapet and spatters the broken earth around me with a hail of rounds. Crouching low I ran with my Chauchat to the next traverse and then popped up in search of targets, and finding several send the rest of my magazine out toward the encroaching line of the enemy. As I ducked down to change out my magazine a few poilus ran past me, some armed and some not but all seemingly in this fight. I heard a commotion off to my left, and so ran a few paces that way before again bringing my weapon up to bear; and that's when I saw what at first I couldn't understand and then secondly couldn't believe. To the left of my position the trench had been reduced to a series of interlocked shell holes— the original structure had all but been obliterated and was even now only still formidable due to the belts of wire that were left uncut during the bombardment. My men were fighting from these holes, their guns resting on the lips of the craters while their bodies lay down inside for cover. There was a small firefight going on between a series of adjacent holes in front of my line that were occupied alternately by German soldiers and my men, when suddenly I saw what could only be fire spout forth from the German hole and fly through the air into the hole occupied by my men. As I stood there rubbing my eyes in disbelief the screams of my men were still audible despite the distance and the cacophony that was going on around me. Am I seeing this correctly? Are the Germans producing a living flame and using it against us? For the moment I was frozen as this horror played out a few hundred meters in front of me. Then, in a flash a group of figures emerged from the ground and rushed past the smoldering crater toward what at the moment constituted the edge of our lines. Shaken from my lethargy I rose my weapon to fire, when all of a sudden a most violent ball of flame erupted from where the German soldiers once were and in the process sent a plume of oily black smoke up into the air like a grotesque balloon. I could only surmise that a round had struck whatever infernal machine the German soldiers were carrying and ignited its fuel, for once the fireball subsided there was nothing left of the team of men but blackened debris. Shouts of defiance flew up all down the line as we shifted our focus back out to shell holes and craters that were filling up with Germans in front of us.

By now, I was down to just two magazines for the Chauchat and was starting to do the frantic mental weapons inventory that a soldier always does in these situations; Chauchat plus two 20-round magazines. Lebel rifle over my shoulder with a full 10-round tube plus some rounds in my pouches. My loaded pistol. My nail. My fists...I made the snap decision to run back to my right to check on my improvised machine gun team, as I knew that if they had been knocked out I would be in great danger of losing this position. Along my journey back to their position I ran past a wooden crate that had been knocked open by the bombardment and was now laying on its side against the wall of the trench. Why I didn't notice it before I can only chock up to the confusion of the situation. Stooping over it briefly I realized that it was full of petard raquettes'—oh these stupid things, what a poor excuse for a hand grenade. At least these were the model that was self-priming, which is good, since at the moment no one had any time to smoke a pipe. After hesitating briefly, I grabbed a handful of them to rush over to the men in the machine gun team to help bolster their position, and clipped one on my belt too for good measure. I arrived to find them still in action minus two men; one nursing a graze wound to the face and the other lying face down in a gory mess. They quickly report to me that they are running low on ammo for the machine gun but still have ammo for their rifles, and with that I saluted them, handed over the raquettes, and ran back from the direction I came. My heart was pounding in my ears now, and I was dizzy with thirst. Crash! Crash! Two German grenades go off in rapid succession in front of my position, showering me with dirt and knocking me down to the ground. With ringing ears, I struggle back to my feet and do a quick onceover—the gun's okay, I'm okay. Knowing in my heart that I must stand my ground and may even die trying I jumped back onto the firestep ready to deal with whatever was waiting for me on the other side of the wire. And what was waiting for me was another long burst of machinegun fire that spouted along the parapet in regular little intervals as it traversed from left to right. A gun team must have somehow set up in no-man's land. This cannot stand. They cannot be permitted to remain where they are, wherever they are. Running to my left again I once more took a leap of faith onto the firestep and this time was able to loose some rounds into the attacking host, which by now had been reduced to haphazard teams of men in shell holes firing at our position irregularly. If only I could find those Stokes mortars…as I rose once more to hopefully make the best of my dwindling ammunition I beheld a new curious and terrifying sight. Right out in the middle of this firefight stands what must be the largest German soldier I have ever seen. He stands right up out of his shell hole to reveal that he is carrying a heavy machinegun all by himself. A MG 08/15. Himself. Before I can even question the dynamics of this, he starts walking foreword, firing long bursts as he goes. What a terrible weapon the German MG 08/15 is, it is capable of firing nearly continuously and seems to be able to find you no matter how far away you are. And right now I am not very far away at all. Here he comes, he's a hundred meters out and is laying down such terrific fire that it is keeping us all at bay. And then it dawns on me—he's covering for the rest of them! If he keeps us all down and defenseless then they can spring up and walk right over us! There is nothing, literally nothing coming from my right now, he's either killed the whole gun team or has them pinned. Seventy-five meters now, and he's still coming, I can see coal scuttles lining the lip of the hole behind him, they will spring forth any minute now and be here before I can organize any sort of resistance. They will surely kill without question every one of us once they get here too, as this has been a bitter gunfight with heavy losses on both sides. Sixty meters now, the bullets from his gun hiss and pop as they whine over me. I somehow manage to worm my way out to a spot where I'm mostly covered but can still bring my weapon to bear. He cannot see me. Fifty meters now. He's paused at a stretch of uncut wire, and is yelling back for pioneers with cutters while still laying down fire. Then I hear it. *Click!* He's reached the end of his drum magazine! Just as quickly as he reached into his bag for the next one I propped myself up on one elbow and shouldered my Chauchat to let fly a perfect stream of rounds at him. He went down like a ton of bricks, hit square in the chest with the last of my ammunition. The immense weight of his MG crumpled him immediately, yet he didn't make it all the way to the ground: His body fell only a short distance before becoming ensnared in the belt of wire that had arrested his momentum in the first place. He now hung there grotesquely like a puppeteer's toy, his body twisted by the awesome weight of his equipment and the various straps around his body used to support it. With his arms spread wide and his head forced back he now stared at me in death, the twisted look of pain forever etched on his face. Even now he still seemed immense, and a shudder ran down my spine as I contemplated alternative outcomes to this scenario. But this was no time for rest! Laying my trusty Chauchat down I slung my rifle around and prepared to do my best with what I had left, when it dawned on me that nothing was happening. Fire had again erupted forth from our lines and I was glad to hear that my machinegun team was still in action, but the back of the German attack seemed to be broken. The massed coal scuttles on the lip of the crater were gone, and no more German grenades sailed through the air. That must have been their last dice throw! They are in retreat! A spontaneous cheer went up all along my tattered line as defiant men stood to full height and took pot-shots at our fleeing foe. One smart-ass somewhere on the line even hurled a raquette out toward the German lines only to have it burst harmlessly out in the smoking mud before our position. I rose slowly, painfully, and limped back over to my little machinegun crew. One more man was down and the man with the face wound had died, but those who were left were as happy and defiant and they were exhausted and scared. It was going to take a lot of work to put this trench back together. *A lot*. But just then French voices could be heard from behind us. What were reinforcements would now become a work party, and I breathed a breath of relief as I slung my rifle and slumped against the wall of the trench. Relieving myself I then found an unbroken cigarette in my pocket and smoked it.

But that was all yesterday. Today, I sip coffee and enjoy extra hot rations with an actual piece of chocolate on the side. We survivors are being rewarded with the morning off and decent food for defending this position and now get to nurse our wounds and watch the work details detached to us repair the wreckage around us. Interestingly enough what started out as crews of French soldiers have been replaced by gangs of Annamites overseen by French NCO's. I suppose by now every Frenchman that can hold a rifle is needed somewhere up and down the line, and so the government has had to reach out to some of the far-flung regions of the Empire for manpower. In any case, they are doing remarkable work. After our artillery pounded the shit out of the German position to start our day, the boches are mostly quiet and seem content to just let us put ourselves back together after yesterday's little stunt. The only thing I've been tasked with today is organizing a burial detail-unpleasant work on any occasion but made worse here today by the ferocity of yesterday's bombardments. Heavy artillery stirs up the rats and destroys their hovels, which drives them out into the open and onto the host of fresh corpses that have been buried, reburied, and dismembered by the artillery. We've chased off or killed the rats that we can get our hands on but for the German soldiers dead in front of our position I'm afraid that they are being devoured today. Most disturbingly, the huge fellow with the MG hanging on the wire in front of our position is providing a gruesome display this afternoon. His already bloated corpse is blackened with flies who fly up in clouds as the rats scurry about him and tear great holes in his cadaver. First of course to go was his face: his fair features are now gone, the rats having gouged out his eyes and torn off his cheeks. His jaw now hangs agape as the disgusting creatures crawl in and out of his throat—they are literally eating him from the inside out. He looks like a scarecrow undulating in the breeze as his now tattered uniform flutters in strips off of his outstretched arms. I haven't decided whether to allow this revolting display to continue or to order the spectacle destroyed by either mortar fire or grenades. The only thing really preventing me from doing so is that his body rests on a particularly intact section of wire, and it would be a shame to have to restring it if it was damaged by our own explosions. So for now this macabre puppet dances before our position while I sip hot coffee and rub my sore elbow. Soon I'll have to make some decisions here about burials and again the question will arise what to do about him. Maybe by then he'll already be reduced to a skeleton in rags which isn't so bad all things considered.

# Chapter Fourteen
## Les Allemands

How many times can you get drunk in a row? How many times until it isn't fun anymore—until it isn't even possible? Our week of leave very quickly devolved into a giant, weeklong bender, which in itself I guess wouldn't have been so bad. But for some reason our seven day drinking party very quickly developed a sinister undertone as the days and nights wore on and then started to blend together. We of course had all gotten pretty blotto our first night here and together shared in the misery the next day in our shared rented room. But almost immediately Lars set out to get drunk again, and by day three he was regularly on the verge of blacking out by evening. He was belligerent, even violent, and got us kicked out of more than a few cafes and pubs. He also became increasingly abusive toward Rolf, to the point where I had to intervene on several occasions, once even physically (though Lars was so drunk that when I grabbed him by the shoulders and spun him around he simply fell to the floor and passed out). Something definitely was very, very wrong with my friend. On the fourth afternoon of our leave, he announced that he felt that we all needed some space and then promptly got up and walked out of the door to our room without further comment. He didn't return back until sometime in the night, long after Rolf and I had gone to bed, and he stunk so fiercely when he did that I thought that he had somehow gotten back into the trenches. He then spent the better part of the night keeping us awake as he alternated between vomiting into a wooden bucket and then passing back out on the floor. Several times I was afraid that he was going to choke, and I wondered to myself if he would still be listed as 'killed in combat' if he were to choke on his own vomit in a rented room in Metz. Things finally had come to a head the next day at breakfast.

"Hey Rolf, Rolf, lend me a few Marks alright? I'm running a little low, and um, I'll buy us a round next time we're out, okay?" I just stared at Lars as I sipped my awful cup of roasted chicory coffee (none of us could afford the real stuff). He looked terrible; his eyes were sunken and bloodshot and his skin was sallow. He looked like he hadn't dragged a razor across his face since we got out here either, and of course there was the aforementioned smell. The sight of Rolf squirming in his chair as Lars badgered him for money was more than I could take this morning. I forcefully slammed my coffee cup down on the table and pushed myself back in my chair. "What the fuck is wrong with you man? How are you already out of money? And what the hell is going on with you? Have you looked in a mirror lately?"

My rapid-fire questions caused him to stop and stare at me as a menacing look began to creep across his furrowed brow. "Oh, I'm sorry. I didn't realize that I needed to report to you. Are you the officer on duty this morning? Okay, um, (he had shot to his feet and was now standing at attention, but was using the most exaggerated movements to salute and was mocking me with his comical tone) let's see. Last evening I was engaged in a small local sortie, in which I was obliged to drink beer and schnapps with a room full of strangers in a hall I didn't recognize. I then finding their company distasteful after a time removed myself to an alley with said schnapps and rather quickly became engaged in a dice game with a new set of strangers. After some time, having lost a goodly portion of my money, I begged of these fellows my leave and set out in search of something inexpensive to eat, as I was hungry and very drunk. Along the way I encountered a rather haggard looking Polish woman in a doorway who turned out to be a prostitute, and who convinced me that I would rather spend some time with her than go and find a meal. Agreeing, I proceeded with her to her den of vice, where for the remaining money I had in my pocket we together chewed a small quantity of Bayer heroin tablets before I then proceeded to bend her over an old chair and fuck her with all my might. Upon finishing, I removed myself from said premises and made my way back here, with some difficulty I'm afraid, and then passed the night rather indisposed with you fine fellows."

I felt as if I were a statue—as if I were made of stone. I just stared at him without changing my expression or saying anything for what seemed like an eternity. I was literally stunned into silence and inactivity. I felt like I was staring at my father after I'd caught him in my sister's room. I couldn't move and he knew it, knew that he could just push past me and that I wouldn't say a word to mother. That I would help clean things up and not say a word to mother. Not until much later…seeing this, and thereby seeing that he was winning at playing the bully, Lars smiled a deep, disgusting smile, saluted wildly as if finished with his ludicrous report, and then sat back down and turned as if he was going to pick up where he left off in harassing Rolf. Luckily I regained my composure before he was able to really begin. "Holy shit, Lars! Are you kidding? You spent the last of your money—money that was to last for a week—on a prostitute last night?"

He spun in his chair to face me and cut me off before I could continue. "No asshole, not just on a prostitute. On drinking, gambling, heroin, *and* a prostitute." I suddenly wanted to hit him. To hit him and then kick him when he was down. I was so disgusted by his presence right now that I couldn't see straight. I felt myself begin to rise in my chair, and as I did so the smirk disappeared from Lars' face. I felt myself growing before him; my pulse began to quicken, my breathing increased, and for the moment the headache I had been nursing all morning was gone. We locked eyes, and as we did so he began to rise in his seat as well. Was there no stopping? Must it come to this? How could I want to, *need* to hurt the man I have cared for since the day we met? We were both very rapidly hurtling toward a collision, both coiling like snakes before a strike. Sweat beaded on my brow. He slowly began to ball his fists. I stepped back from the table, pushing my chair back as I did so. The tension in the air was as palpable as it was unbearable. At this point, any move by either of us would set things in motion, terrible things that would be impossible to stop. I unclasped the little leather keeper on the sheath of my jagdnicker though as I did so nausea crept up the back of my throat…

*Crunch!* At that very moment Rolf, who had been sitting quietly through all of this, chose to bite into a piece of rock-hard toasted bread that had been sitting on a plate in front of him this entire time. The noise he made when doing so was so startling that it momentarily shook both Lars and I out of our standoff. But it was the noises he made next that changed the nature of the confrontation. As mentioned before, poor Rolf had such a difficult time eating now, on account of him biting a goodly portion of his tongue off during the bombardment. To what extent his other mouth injuries were I am not aware, but when he ate it sometimes was a rather hideous spectacle. This morning's bread proved nearly impossible to eat for anyone who dared try and for poor

Rolf it was nearly his undoing. In order to make any headway, he was forced to chew with his mouth full open, and as he did so he emanated the most repellent noises while at the same time flung drool and spittle all over himself. Admittedly it was an unsavory spectacle but it caused Lars to fly into a rage. He recoiled from Rolf in horror and put his hands over his ears, as if the sounds of eating were physically injuring him. He actually stumbled over his chair from trying to get away so fast. For the second time in as many minutes, my friend Lars had me staring at him in frozen disbelief. "Ahh! God! Stop! No! No! I can't take it, shut your goddamn mouth when you chew! Shut it! Shut it!" He was actually shrieking. He looked like a new recruit who's just put his hand through a corpse for the first time while diving for cover into a shell hole. "You, you're disgusting! Don't you ever make that noise by me again!" At that, Lars knocked over his chair as he stumbled away from our table and set off down the alley that lead back out onto the street. Now he was gone. Gone without a papiermark in his pocket and wearing the vomit-stained clothes that he passed out in the night before on the floor of our room. And poor Rolf, sitting there stunned and ashamed. Again I saw in him the hurt little boy at the dinner table, but before I could say anything to him he rose from the table and walked a little ways away, trying his best to compose himself as Lars had made him cry again. What the hell was wrong with my friend?

What was wrong with my friend? My friend. My beautiful, charming, selfless friend. The words 'my friend' echoed in my head like the sound of a pebble being kicked down a long tiled hallway. He was turning, *had* turned into a monster. But why? We have been through more or less the same set of horrible things since meeting in those early days, and both suffered through the monstrous bombardment during our work detail. Was it his face wound I wondered? I have repeatedly reassured him that he still was very handsome and that in time his scars would fade. Was he angry with me? Angry for not protecting him, for not sheltering him during those terrible moments? I don't really know how I could have done more, and to be fair I was rather hurt myself. Was it because I have insisted that we befriend Rolf and that we take him with us on our leave? He is harmless, and has certainly not caused Lars any lasting issue. My mind reeled with all of these questions and more, and my heart began to feel so *heavy*. It was killing me to watch my relationship with him fall apart, and was so very hurt by the things he was doing and saying. It was like he was a completely different person after our ordeal that day and frankly, he was beginning to scare me.

That morning could I guess be considered the low point of our leave if one was determined to identify one. From that day on, Lars was scarce; he slept in our room every night but then was for the most part gone once we woke up. His physical appearance continued to deteriorate as the rest of the week wore on and by the last day he literally looked like he had been back up to the front. As he came and went we rarely exchanged more than pleasantries and he never divulged where had been or where he was headed to next. I shuddered to think what he had been doing for money, or how he was feeding himself, and had all but given up on the idea that he was going to pay his share of the room once it was time to settle up and head back to the train station. In the meantime, Rolf and I had passed quiet afternoons in the cafes around the Place Saint-Louis, sometimes chatting with other soldiers but never really befriending any. We did on occasion take to drink as well and I for one began to acquire a taste for red wine, but we never got out of control and always kept to ourselves. Besides, I knew that I needed to set aside enough Papiermarks to settle the bill for the room and for a train ticket back to the front—and more than likely one for Lars, too.

When the last day came, I found myself a little overcome with emotion—emotions that swirled and churned inside of me. I was angry, sad, lonely, anxious, lost. I wanted to go. I wanted to stay. I wanted some semblance of normalcy in my life again—and found it appalling to think that being back up in our trenches could somehow provide it. Rolf was despondent too, and furthermore both of us were anxious to see what version of Lars we were going to get for our journey back, or even if we were going to see him at all. That morning I woke to find that of course, on our last day, Lars had chosen to not come back to our room the night before. After a quick search that turned up nothing, Rolf and I decided to skip breakfast and to set about packing our things and settling up the bill with the landlord. He wasn't at his desk when we rang for him, but his teenage son was there cleaning up the foyer when we arrived. He took one look at us and then set aside his broom, holding up one finger and saying "*attends ici*" as he walked to his father's desk to retrieve an envelope. He then walked over and handed me the envelope and upon opening it I found a note addressed to us:

*Bill for room # 4*

*22 Francs (6.55 papiermark) per day for 6 Days = 132 Francs (39.30 papiermark)*

*Extra fee for mess, damages, and disturbances = 15 Francs (4.45 papiermark)*

*Thank You*

I showed to the note to Rolf, whose brow furrowed the same as mine did when he read it; not only was Lars not going to help pay for our room but he had managed to earn us an almost *5 Mark* fine for his bullshit behavior. We both rummaged around in our pockets and managed to come up with almost the exact bill (in papiermarks) which I then handed to the landlord's son along with the letter back. He took a moment to count our money, then folded our payment along with the letter back into an envelope and stuck it in a desk drawer. Without even as much as casting us another glance he then turned and walked back over to his broom, murmuring a half-hearted '*au revoir*' as he picked it back up and resumed his sweeping. I guess we had worn out our welcome more than I had realized. Without further ado (and not a little glad that we didn't run into the actual landlord) we picked up our things and headed back up to our room. Once we got there we were greeted by the spectacle of Lars stretched out on my cot and fast asleep—asleep with his filthy uniform on right down to his boots.

"Lars! Lars, it's good to see you. Hey, you've got to get up. Wake up, wake up. We have to go, our passes expire today. We've already checked out of the…" He turned his head to look at me and opened his eyes, or rather, his right eye, as his left eye was blackened and swollen nearly shut. "Good morning to you too, Kurt. Nice to see that you were going to abandon me here." With that, and somewhat to my surprise, he slowly and painfully sat up in my cot and began casting about for his belongings. It became readily apparent that some of his things were no longer in his sea bag, which I took to understand that he had either been robbed or had hawked some his belongings to get by over these last few days. In either case, he was mumbling to himself as he hastily packed what was left of his things. I was personally curious to see whether he had managed to preserve enough of his kit to present a proper soldier upon our return, and also began to wonder whether he still had his Iron

Cross as I imagined that a soldier could easily trade one for drink, or worse. "Okay, I'm ready. Are you guys ready? Hi Rolf." Rolf shot him a cold glance, yet I could tell that he was more afraid of Lars than anything and so still ended up smirking a little in order to not appear as ready for a confrontation.

The walk back to the train station resembled little of the triumphant march that the three of us had made in coming the other way just a week ago—save for the shuttered and barren shops and the sullen people that we passed along the way. Lars looked like a monster, and anyone who caught his eye quickly turned away with a start. Though admittedly there were few that did as he mostly stared at the ground as he staggered along and mumbled to himself. In contrast, Rolf still looked smart in his uniform and I suppose I did as well, both of us still sporting our Iron Crosses and myself still wearing my little jagdnicker on my belt. We almost looked like two soldiers escorting a deserter back to the officer on duty and the image in my mind made me chuckle aloud as we plodded along. As we grew closer to the train station we began to encounter other groups of soldiers heading that way as well, along with fresh groups of soldiers excitedly heading the other way to begin what we had just finished. It struck me that Lars wasn't the only one to look like he had just lost a battle: many of the soldiers returning looked penniless and hungover—some even appeared wounded while still others needed assistance just to walk down the street. The best that I could reckon was that either the vice in this city was such that it readily sucked a good man down and destroyed both his health and his morals in the process, or Metz was slowly exacting her punishment for the War of 1870 on us one German soldier at a time. In any case, it looked as if Metz had easily gotten the better hand in this latest round. As I went to turn and say something to Rolf suddenly the long, low moan of a train whistle came floating over us from the direction that we were headed. How sorrowful it sounded! Hearing the train in the distance caused my emotions to stir while sending a shiver down my spine. I couldn't help but picture Lars and I walking to the train station for the first time as newly minted soldiers, excited to be being sent to the front and convinced that we were lucky to be chosen to participate in this adventure. In my mind's eye, Lars and I appeared to be children, and in many ways we were. Laughing and horsing around and boasting to each other and all who would hear about our prowess in all things related to manhood. Yet I could also remember Lars falling asleep during one of the many interminable delays along the way, his head falling to the side and coming to rest on my shoulder...

Yes, it was all coming back to me now. The boyish naivety, the excitement, the fear, the innocence, the innocence lost. The war. The train platform...Not long after hearing the train we turned the corner and saw the train. Or rather the train stopped next to the train station with its platform and large plaza full of milling soldiers. Milling soldiers and Feldgendarmerie. I glanced over at Lars and found him sweating bullets and glancing around like a wounded animal. Either he was coming down from something or was genuinely terrified to run into any number of individual chained dogs who might be looking for him. As the crowd thickened around us we found ourselves being funneled into one of several lines that terminated at a wall of Feldgendarmerie that separated the crowd of soldiers from the waiting train at the siding. Soldiers were having their passes examined and in some cases their sea bags as well before being allowed to proceed to the officers seated at long tables who were stamping the passes. Then it was onto the train to await the long ride back to the front. As we were being herded closer to the front of the line I could make out that some soldiers were being given a hard time for this or that, either their appearance or their paperwork not being in order. I even heard a soldier be forcibly removed from the line and watched him get hauled off by two huge Feldgendarmerie goons. As I could clearly see that Lars was on the verge of collapse I reached out and put my hand on his shoulder, and asked him in as pleasant a tone as I could muster if everything was okay. "Huh? Oh, yeah, huh, yeah, I'm okay. Sure. Why? Why do you ask?"

"Oh, only because you look like you're going to faint. I'm just worried about you is all. Is there anything I can do?" I was really laying it on here, as what I really wanted to ask him was whether or not there was any *particular* reason for the chained dogs up ahead to want to beat his ass once we got up to their line and they recognized his face. I was almost convinced at this point that he had either done something very wrong and was being sought for it or had something that didn't belong in his sea bag in his sea bag.

"Papers! Fine! Next. Papers! Hold on, what's this then. Fine. Next. Papers! What? Get yourself cleaned up. Next..." We were being fed through the wall of Feldgendarmerie like a belt through a MG 08, each soldier passing through like a numberless round before disappearing into the crowd on the train. We were close enough to hear the proceedings, and to me they didn't sound too thorough. Maybe if Lars could just play it cool and keep his head down we could pass through this without incident. Before long, it was our turn. "Next!" A large bewhiskered Sergeant took my leave papers from me and then asked to see my identification disk. He then gave me a quick once-over before grunting his approval and bidding me to proceed. As there were other groups of soldiers milling around who were obviously waiting for comrades to be processed, I simply walked a few paces and then turned around to await the fate of my two friends. Or rather, my one friend, as before I was really even settled Rolf came striding toward me with a relieved look on his face (though I couldn't fathom why he'd have anything to fear). We then both got to observe with growing concern the large Sergeant begin to give Lars the hard time that we had all feared. "Halt! What is this? A soldier in the Imperial German Army in such a pitiful state? Where is your feldmutze? Who blackened your eye?" Lars appeared to be melting like a pat of lard in a skillet before this increasingly agitated Feldgendarmerie. He put his hand on Lars' shoulder and motioned for some goons to take him away, which was more than I was prepared to witness and which caused me to pipe up more than I probably should have. "Sir! This man is my friend. I can vouch for his…"

"Enough! If he is your friend then you must be trouble too, both of you, be off!" As the Sergeant turned and returned to his work two giant chained dogs made clear that we were to follow them. Lars said nothing. I cleared my throat. Rolf tagged along and no one seemed to notice.

We were led into what probably was a small office of some sort before the war, but was now serving as the place of final judgement for soldiers returning from leave under sordid conditions. The three of us were bade to stand before a large wooden table, our hands folded behind our backs, while the goons stood against the wall behind us with our belongings. It all had the feel of an impromptu firing squad and if it weren't for the fact that the goons were *behind* us I would have started to become worried. There were voices from down the hall that led away from the table before us, when at once a frowsy, graying and pallid officer appeared before us with our leave papers in his hands. Or rather, his hand, as the empty pinned sleeve of his uniform betrayed his loss from another war. Though he still had a proud air about him his face showed every strain of a constitution that never fully recovered from his ordeals, and the faded decorations on his crumpled uniform bore witness to the fact that nonetheless the Empire had appreciated his sacrifices. We three saluted sharply (even Lars) before he sat down in an old wooden chair and glared at us before laying our passes on the table. "I am Feldwebel Schulz, and I am sorry to see three stupid Bavarian soldiers standing before me here who should be instead boarding a train and heading back up to where the fighting is. Yes, all three of you are stupid. You because you are a fuck up, and you other two for being his friend and making excuses for him." We all knew very well where we fit into his neat equation, and I only wondered if at this point I was going to find out just exactly how much trouble Lars was actually in. There was a long and uncomfortable pause as the Feldwebel's words died away in my head, while all the while the tension in the air clung to us palpably. Then the unexpected happened. "You three, sit down." He then let out a long sigh as he rubbed his face and tired eyes with his hand. "I know why you joined the army. You joined for the same exact reasons that I did: We were at war with France, I wanted to seem brave, I wanted to have an adventure, and I wanted to get laid. And all these things I did and more, and I can suppose the same is true for you three."

At this, the tiniest of smirks briefly crept across Lars' face and stuck around just long enough for me to notice. Rolf looked dumbfounded. "Brave boys! Brave boys indeed. I see that all three of you have been wounded, I too, was wounded once…" He obviously didn't need to point out his wound, but he leaned slightly foreword with his empty sleeve anyway as his voice seemed to trail off in thought. Then he straightened up and the Prussian Officer returned. "You three must know that this war is far from over, must know that you are still needed in this fight, and must know just as well that you belong to the Kaiser and his Armies until the war is finished or it is finished with you. Now I can do anything I want with you three, I can even have you shot. But I want to think that you will be more useful back up at the front, even if it's just to stop a French bullet or bayonet." There was that old German army camaraderie that we'd been missing. I couldn't help but laugh too because the last time I saw a bayonet it was German and was in the process of being ground down by a pioneer into a fighting knife—the last French one I saw was stuck in the side of a trench and being used as a nail to hold a small mirror on a string. No one fought with bayonets anymore. "Now I'm going to stamp all three of these passes, despite the deplorable condition that you are in (Glaring at Lars), and expect you to grab your gear and get your asses on that train without further incident. The stamp of this office is different than the standard stamp, and carries with it a promise—that if any of you get out of line again and find yourself at the mercy of another Feldgendarmerie your stamp will be discovered and you will be promptly shot out of hand." With that, he stamped all three of our passes in bright red ink and then bade the goons behind us to take us away. The last I saw of this sad little relic was him closing his ink pad and then adjusting the epaulette and braid on his empty sleeve. Thrust back into the sunlight we three were free to go and apparently try to die for our country again.

As we were funneled into the herd and then incrementally into the train the entire experience we had just endured began to finally register on my brain. At first blush, it would seem as if the three of us had been given a reprieve, at least partially because of the fact that we had been previously decorated for being wounded. On second thought though the idea struck me that perhaps we were only being spared because the empire was running out of soldiers. These thoughts and more were rattling around in my brain as we were compelled into our seats by the crush of the crowd. Apparently this train was to be filled to standing room only before we departed. As I adjusted my bag before me and took one last look out the window at dirty little Metz Lars was the first to speak. "That was some speech by our Grossvater there, wasn't it? And to think, he's dipped his little pecker in a madchen before too!"

"Fuck you, Lars." Lars just laughed at me and settled back into his chair in preparation of falling asleep, and I almost wanted to switch spots so that I could sit next to him.

# Chapter Fifteen
# Die Franzosen

It is all hearsay, of course, but what really isn't hearsay these days? No one man knows anything for sure, he just talks confidently when he likes what he is talking about. Rumors, gossip, bullshit. This is all the frontline soldier knows. I for one haven't seen a proper newspaper in quite some time either, only scraps of the frontline trench papers that are printed up in jest and circulated until someone ends up using the paper for something more important than reading. Yet I've heard the same rumor now several times over the last several days, and it's starting to grow on me. Parts of it I know and believe: The war is at a standstill. Neither Germany nor France are strong enough to defeat the other. England is running out of men, and her Empire is starting to falter. It's the other part of the rumor that has me intrigued—America may be joining the war. The United States of America. They of course would be joining the war effort on our side, too, and if so naturally would contribute enough men to defeat Germany if by nothing other than sheer numbers. How wonderful. Though why the United States would possibly want to join this awful war seems beyond me, and further seems beyond anyone who is engaged in spreading the rumor. Certainly no one has attacked her, and I don't believe she has any colonies to defend. Plus I find it kind of hard to believe that the United States would want to fight on the same side as England in a conflict, given their history. Then again, it is fantastic to think that France and England would ever fight on the same side of any conflict but maybe we did in the Crimea, so I suppose miracles do happen. But this is just a rumor of course. What is a fact is that our army seems incapable of mounting an offensive; most of the veterans from the early days of the conflict having been killed or disabled and what's now coming in to fill their places are either young boys or old men. Then too, just the whole nature of the conflict now has made it impossible to mount a major offensive. The Boches haven't really done so for more than a year now and I suppose that we haven't either. We just whittle away at each other as if we were two great woodsmen set on opposing stumps, each of us daily chipping away at the other in order to see who will fall of their perch first. The huge stunt that the boches opposite pulled some time back has been the last real push they have given us, and constitutes the last time that I was close enough to a German soldier to see his face—dead or alive. So really I suppose it would take a new player in this great game to make any real or major change in the daily proceedings, which is why I believe America's name has been thrown around so much as of late. They are really the last great nation that isn't involved and that could make a difference one way or the other.

But what I know of Americans is not good; that they are lazy, rich, over proud, and only interested in fighting with their fists. They would be eaten alive if they came here and had to live with the rats in these rotten trenches and endure the daily hate and random murder. This is why I consider them coming as just another rumor, albeit an intriguing one. I have been to several officer's calls in the last week—officer's calls that now habitually include NCOs over the rank of Caporal—that have all been chiefly concerned with the morale and fighting spirit of the men. I always report the same; that the men in my section are either new and scared shitless or old and indifferent, and that under no circumstances do I believe that this section is capable of mounting a coordinated or sustained attack on the lines directly in front of us. In delivering reports like this I used to wince, as generally frankness of this sort is not tolerated by high command and could even result in charges of insubordination. But now it is accepted as scripture and generally without comment. It would seem as if even the old bemedaled heroes back in their headquarters are starting to run out of the strength necessary to carry on for much longer. Either that, or all the old breed of officers that we started out with have now been killed off and then replaced with a new crop of men, men whose attitudes better reflect the pessimism and hopelessness that is the war now. As a coda to the pervading apathy drinking and sloppy behavior in general has become the norm again in this sector as it both sustains the grizzled and calms the new. I for one have been putting away pinard at a rate that has far outstripped my daily supply, which has caused me to have to make certain arrangements in order to be able to enjoy my luxurious lifestyle. In fact, if it weren't for the incessant officer's calls lately I would probably be hard pressed to even keep up with myself, given that I make it a point to at least be halfway sober when I attend one.

But today, I went completely sober. Not out of a burning sense of duty or an overarching sense of shame, but rather, because I am bone dry. No matter though, as I have plans to leave the meeting when dismissed and proceed directly to where today's hot rations are to be picked up later. I have arranged to meet a man there about acquiring more and whatever else I might think of once I'm there. Yes, today I was completely sober when I stood before my Capitaine and was handed an envelope that was sealed and addressed to me. Had I been fortified with drink I probably would have not broken out in sweat and began to tremble upon its receipt. "Ha ha! Sergent you shake like a leaf! This is precisely why this is being handed to you. Go ahead, open it." As if in slow motion I slid my greasy finger along the sealed edge, tearing the envelope methodically as I inched from right to left. I was convinced I was being handed plans for an offensive. Or was being ordered to a new sector. Or being arrested. I let my eyes fall to the page before focusing, which gave the effect of the words rising to the surface like fish in a pond. "Sir? Am I to understand that I am being given 48 hours leave? Is this correct?" I was shocked. I hadn't been away from the front entirely for over a year.

"Yes, Sergent, you are being given a reprieve. Partly because of your gallant defense of this sector recently, and partly because high command wants to reward those with long service with some rest. You have not been given permission to leave this district however so I'm afraid that Paris is out of the question, but I'm sure that you will find Reims relaxing. Plus I heard that American officers have set up a club there, perhaps you can tell them some war stories, eh?" With that we saluted and then I parted. As I walked away from the command dugout I at first staggered as if drunk, yet my pace seemed to quicken with every step and I couldn't tell if it was because I was excited or because I was half expecting a German shell to prematurely end my good fortune at any moment. By the time I was more than a few paces away, I was hurrying along at such a clip that I even forgot about my rendezvous for pinard, and I don't even think I thought about it until I was back in my dugout trying to pack my seabag. No matter. There would be plenty to drink with the Americans in Reims. Americans? I'll be damned—the fools have come after all.

Leaving this sector that I have called home for so long was like being reborn—I felt as if I was being forced out of a womb and into a frightening new world in which I didn't seem or want to belong. The camion ride away from the front was monotonous until we joined the traffic on the widened country road headed west toward Reims. I was bewildered by all the hustle and crush of humanity that was coursing through the countryside as the clumsy camion that I was riding in swayed and lurched its way through the endless file of vehicles and our Annamite driver swore at it all in his savage tongue. I had never seen so many automobiles in my life! Camions full of all sorts of things; boxes and crates, soldiers and livestock, fruit, hay, coffins. This all gave the roadway an air of a gypsy parade and made me feel like so much war materiel. I knew no one in the camion in which I was riding and spoke nothing as I gazed blankly at the horizon toward which we travelled. I couldn't stop myself from checking my wristlet incessantly, either. I wanted a drink. My back hurt. The air in the camion was foul. A soldier near me wept more or less continually. Our Annamite driver swore at the traffic. I wound my wristlet. What would Reims be like? I found that I didn't as much care that I was headed to a city as I was anxious to take a bath. They could have given me leave to sit in a bathtub ten minutes behind the lines and I would have been happy. In fact, now that the shock of being given some leave had worn off I didn't much relish the thought of having to interact with other drunken poilus and endure their boastful war stories—and I was not at all excited at the prospect of meeting the Americans.

I was jarred back into reality when I realized just how close Reims was to the German front. We had been travelling as best as I could tell due west but as the road started to drift northward the sounds of shelling could be heard once more. The signs on the side of the roadway indicated we were not far from the city, yet the countryside was rather continuously pock marked with artillery craters and even the occasional pile of detritus. Just what kind of leave was this to be? Despite being dressed in my only off duty uniform I still wore my pistol belt and suddenly I felt compelled to check that all was in order—as if we suddenly came under a bombardment my pathetic little sidearm would be of any use. Those around me seemed rather taken aback as well, and a general murmur arose amongst the poilus as concern turned to anger at the prospect of being told one thing and given quite another. Presently the vehicle in front of us slowed to a crawl, and it was sometime before I realized that the reason why was because the road had been obliterated by some fairly heavy shelling up ahead. The sudden knowledge that the boches had this road zeroed in at one time or another made me feel rather uneasy, and as our camion trundled off the road and to the right around the crater I found myself glancing skyward and straining for the sound of a shell whining. Which was ridiculous. Clearly the French army wouldn't be moving so much materiel over this road if it wasn't safe to do so. Still…the occasional burned-out hull of a camion off to the side of the road was not reassuring. Again the sounds of shelling came drifting across the fields from off somewhere to our right, causing everyone to jerk their heads so quickly in that direction that we must have looked like a basket of kittens before a child with a string. As I jerked my head right I instinctually put my hands up to grab the sides of my helmet like I've done a million times before—only to be rudely reminded that I was wearing my off-duty kepi, not my Adrian. Great. Now it felt like there was a giant target painted on the top of my head and suddenly more than ever I wanted to get out of this miserable contraption. This was the first time I had ever been inside of a moving vehicle while there was the prospect of coming under attack, and the sensation made me want to jump out and run away. To my estimation it would be infinitely safer to be a small running target than a large trundling one. I checked my wristlet again. Sixteen thirty. The time was insignificant yet for some reason I needed to keep checking it. Finally, finally, the camion in front of us slowed to a crawl, but this time it was because we were approaching the outskirts of Reims.

Or I should say, the picked over remains of the outskirts of Reims. All around us were piles of brick debris and shattered homesteads, dotted here and there with shanties of the remaining inhabitants that were managing to eke out whatever living they could. I was immediately furious. What the fuck *is* this? I was promised a leave! With an officer's club! The camion suddenly lurched as it went over a small crater in the road that was hastily filled in with boards and broken bricks. What the fuck! I wanted out. Now. In fact, I was just building myself up and checking my things in preparation for jumping out over the side of the camion when all traffic stopped and the engine was shut off by the driver (who then promptly nodded off to sleep). Before I knew it, Marechaussee were stalking down both sides of the camion and flinging open the tailgates in a clear sign that it was time for us to disembark. Apparently this was the end of the line. As we more or less lined up on the side of the road a stooped figure of a Gendarmerie Capitaine hobbled before us and demanded our attention. "Soldiers! You are less than a kilometer from Reims, but this is the end of your camion ride. I trust that you will all proceed to the city in an orderly fashion and not overstay your welcome. I will not bother with checking all your passes, the gendarmerie are everywhere and will round up whoever needs a reminder when it's time to go. Listen up! The Americans are training near here and their officers have been known to frequent the city at night. Do not fight with them! Our Gendarmerie will not tolerate such behavior and their Military Police are likely to fight you back. Remember, these men are here because they want to be, they are our allies, and you represent France. Now go." With his somewhat lackluster speech concluded the little creature of a man was helped into a weather-beaten staff car and then was off in a puff of dust and exhaust. How ridiculous.

While the camions puffed and rasped as they labored to turn around and head back whence they came a general exodus began toward the direction in which we had initially been heading. Men slung their bags and began their trek, some beginning to pair up or to form into groups. I for one veered off to the side of the road less travelled and trudged on alone with the pathetic little Capitaine's speech playing back in my head. So what I had heard was doubly true; not only were the Americans here in France but all they wanted to do was get drunk and fight with their fists. Great. As these thoughts went through my mind I began glancing around to not only take in my surroundings but also in the hopes of maybe finding a small café that might be less of an attraction to the crowds. What struck me was that not only were there no little cafes but that there was little of anything—the destruction out on the road was continuing right up into the city. In fact, as the city loomed before me I could plainly see that many of the building were roofless and that the streets were strewn with brick rubble and garbage. I honestly wanted to turn around and run. How on earth was this to be any sort of leave—it was still in the war zone! Just then I caught the faint sound of music over the crunch of my boots on the rubble-strewn macadam. Apparently life went on within these city walls after all. As our little parade of poilus passed through what currently constituted as the city gate we were transported into a world of busy and undaunted life. Through glass-less windows could be seen soldiers sipping drinks and smoking their pipes at broken and dusty tables: the smell of coffee and tobacco smoke drifted through the air as somewhere a gramophone wheezed and a woman laughed.

Here, a boy selling apples out of a wooden bucket. There, a prostituee chatting with a poilu as she ran her hand up his inner thigh. Cigarette butts everywhere. This wasn't so bad after all.

I stopped a man sweeping glass up in the street to get my bearings. "Excuse me. I am looking for a place to have a drink. Can you point me in the right direction? I only have a short time."

"Yes, of course, all of you want a drink and only have a short time. This place here is okay but has mixed company, down the street to the right is the American Officer's club—across the street from it is the French Officer's club. I recommend the American club since they cannot tell who is an officer in the French army and who is not." With that, he turned back to his work, which is when I realized that he was missing most of his left hand. From his age, I had to guess that he was a wounded poilu who came here after his discharge, which would help explain his knowledge of the American Officer's club. I thanked him though he paid me no further mind, and then I was off. As I walked down the street I immediately felt a little sheepish about asking for where to go; there weren't that many standing buildings with complete roofs, and seemingly all the ones that did have them housed some sort of den of vice. Men laughed and sang and fought while prostituees stood smoking cigarettes in every doorway, while all around shattered buildings sagged against one another and stared window-less into the street. What happened here? I momentarily thought to turn around and go back and ask the street sweeper about the destruction but when I glanced back he was gone. Oh well. I was sure that I'd find out soon enough and in the meantime I had a taste for a drink that wasn't Pinard.

Approaching the American club, which was easy to identify due to their colors flying from a makeshift pole in front of it, I was immediately stopped by one of their MP's who was standing at the door. He looked to be about 19, and didn't have a speck of dirt on either his face or his uniform. "Hey you, Frenchy, where you goin'? You speak English? Enn-glish?" I happen to speak English fairly well thanks to the mandatory prep classes I took in school, but at this moment I patently refused to indulge him. "*Excusez-moi. Je suis le lieutentant Cloutier. Je te depasse, alors bouge ton cul pour que je puisse prendre un verre.*" At this, I confidently tapped my Sergent's stripes and then motioned with my eyes to my non-commissioned officer's kepi, and then straightened up as if I expected him to step aside and let me pass. "Oh shit, a General. Um, sorry Sir. Really sorry. Please, come on in." Once he realized the gravity of his error he snapped an extremely stiff salute and stood aside for me to enter. I slung my bag over my shoulder, stared at him coldly and casually returned the salute before stepping across the threshold and into the club. As my senses adjusted to the smoky din the first thing I noticed was the overwhelming stench of perfume, followed closely by wet leather and then alcohol. I then slowly was able to make out that over the murmur of men's voices and the crackle of the gramophone there could be heard the coquettish chitter of flirtatious women. Squinting and looking around I could see that almost every seated officer had either a prostituee on his lap or one standing behind him with her arms wrapped around him and her fingers playing with his uniform buttons. How pathetic! Up at the front poilus were rubbing themselves raw in between attacks (German, rat, or otherwise) while back here safe behind the lines our American cousins—who have only been away from their sweethearts maybe six months at best—are expending all their energies fucking every whore in France! Now I was the one that wanted to fight with my fists. It took me a moment to collect myself, and in the process the pathetic little capitaine's speech again played back in my mind. "Comport yourself so, you represent France." Clearing my throat I then adjusted my kepi and made for the bar.

As I found a spot in between sets of flirting Yankees I was astounded to find that the man keeping bar was a Frenchman. As he was in between orders I was able to snatch a moment of conversation, beginning with, "Does anyone in here speak French?"

"No, not generally. They have all been issued little translation guides but their attempts at communicating are generally abominable. Still, watch what you say, as you never know who may be listening, or who may know a bit of what's going on, Sergent."

With that, he gave me a little wink and then looked around to see if anyone had been listening to our conversation. "Who are you, may I ask? And how is it that you are tending bar for Americans here in Reims?"

"I am the owner of this establishment, which was a country inn before the war. My wife and children have moved out into the countryside but I have decided to stay on here and keep up business as best as I can. The Americans keep me supplied with their whiskies and cigarettes which I then duly sell back to them, and in that I keep up some brisk dealings. If you're looking for a room however all of mine are currently booked I'm afraid, but I can still offer you a hot bath if you'd like to schedule one. As for the working girls, you're on your own there, as I have no contracts with any of them." Amazing. I've come all this way to stand face-to-face with a real live profiteer. I had heard stories up at the front about men who somehow had managed to worm themselves out of active service and to make a handsome Franc in the process, but I have never believed them. Yet here I stand before one in a room full of Americans— sometimes rumors end up being true. In any case, my internal moral dilemma was quickly solved by the fact that this snake had mentioned two things that I desperately needed at the moment—a drink and a bath. "Well, it's a pity about the room, but all the same I will gladly take you up on the offer for a bath. In the meantime, I'll take a—what was it called—a whiskey."

He smiled a little slimy smile at me as he was wiping a glass down with a towel, and as he placed the glass down in preparation to make my drink he first thrust a battered old tablet of paper in front of me. Glancing it over I surmised that this was his ledger that he kept for services at his inn. Finding the column for baths and then glancing at my wristlet (that I was suddenly glad that I had wound so much on the camion) I saw that I'd have to wait over an hour for a bath to free up. No matter I suppose, as I didn't have any plans or anywhere really to go. I supposed that at some point I'd have to worry about securing some lodging but for now my focus was going to have to be sipping whatever whiskey was and then then taking a nice hot bath. "This bath that I'm about to pay for is hot, correct? Because I can always stand out in the cold rain for free." The innkeeper smiled up at me over the brown glass bottle that he had just uncorked and then simply nodded his head as he poured a golden-brown liquid out into the glass before me, stopping about three fingers up. "Let's see. That will be 3 Francs for the whisky, and 5,25 Francs for the bath—5,50 if you need soap and a towel…" His voice trailed off as he looked me over, presumably to see if I had a towel wrapped around me. "So let's call it 8,50 altogether then, okay?"

"8,50! Do you know how much Poilus are getting paid these days? And you want 3 Francs for a drink that isn't even halfway full? I'm a little taken aback that you would gouge a French soldier the same as you would a Yankee." At this, he screwed his face up a little and then leaned over the bar as if he had something really important to tell me. "Look, *Sergent*, first of all I can just as easily let the MP at the door know that you're not an officer as I can sell you this drink, so you need to curb the attitude. Secondly, this is the *only* place in

118

town outside of a private residence—and you don't look like you know anyone in town—for you to take a hot bath. And finally…" as he said 'finally' he held up the drink in front of my face, swirling it a little as he did so. "As for the drink, you don't know what you're talking about. This isn't a glass of pinard. So either pay up and go find a seat, or get your shit together and go find the door. It doesn't matter to me." I really, *really* wanted to hurt this son of a bitch right here and now. Wanted to more than hurt him. It hadn't been long since I'd taken a life and suddenly the lines between the front and this shitty little club were starting to blur in my head. Thankfully I pulled myself together and managed put on a brave face. "Here's your 8,50, *Judas*. Now I'll be over there at that table sipping my drink, do come get me when my bath is ready." At that, I put a pile of greasy money on the bar, maintaining eye contact the entire time as the battered Francs fell from my hand, and then slung my bag and was off, whiskey in hand.

As I shouldered my way through the smoky room full of Yankees and whores I could feel their gaze upon me—presumably for different reasons but I didn't really care. The only thing that bothered me was whether any of them actually spoke French, or could understand our uniform rank system. In any case, I chose to feign indifference as I sat down at a small and wobbly bistro table that was a little away from the crowd along a back wall. Putting my bag down where the second person would sit I clearly displayed that I didn't want company as I sat down myself and put my drink in front of me. Before I took a sip, though I reached into the top of my bag and found my long-neglected pipe and the small leather bag of tobacco that was wound around it. I hadn't taken the time to smoke my pipe in so long and now that I had some time to kill I figured—why not? As I struck a Lucifer and then held it over the bowl I was whisked out of the crowded room by the pleasant taste and aroma of a good smoke—not a shitty Army issue cigarette but a real drag of real tobacco. After a few good puffs, I then gave my whiskey a try. And as it turned out, the snake of an innkeeper was right. This *wasn't* Pinard. Now I've had brandy before, we used to enjoy it around the holidays, and that always packed a bit of a punch. But this, *this* was like drinking fuel. I could literally feel it burning all the way down into my stomach and I honestly worried that if I took another drag of my pipe I'd burst into flames. But all that aside, I could tell it was *strong*. And I liked that. So after a few more sips to get adjusted and a drag of my pipe to dispel my worry about exploding I settled down into my rickety little chair and tried to pretend that I was completely alone.

Which didn't work. Much to my dismay I wasn't a finger into my drink when I caught an American officer walking over to me out of the corner of my eye. Pausing a respectful distance from my table he stopped and snapped a salute, which irritated me to no end because among other things meant that I had to put my pipe and my drink down in order to return it. Doing so, he then approached my table and yet remained at attention. I resumed my smoking and drinking. "Colonel, sir. Do you know if any of your men happen to have any good German loot they'd wish to sell? I'd love to get my hands on a boot knife, or on one of those long Mauser bayonets with the teeth on the back." Pausing, he then adjusted how he was standing and then looked around as if he didn't want anyone to see us talking or to overhear our conversation. For my part, I was at least looking at him. "But what I'd really love to get, would kill for, is one of those spiked leather helmets. You know, a Pickelhaube. P—I—C, 'em, you know, P, for Pickelhaube?" Why on earth he thought spelling it would help me understand what he wanted I could only chalk up to him being drunk. In any case, I knew that he didn't know how to spell Pickelhaube despite knowing what letter it started with. After he was done, he just stood there and stared at me, too, which was not only annoying but was also rude. Clearly he was waiting to see if I understood English, and at this juncture I decided that I didn't. "*Si vous etes si interesse par les Allemands, puis-je suggerer que vous montiez reellement au front et que vous vous battiez? Je peux vous assurer que vous verrez beaucoup d'Allemends a ce moment-la, et je suis sur que certains d'entre eux seraient heureux de vous aider dans votre chasse au tresor.*" Just as I suspected, he did not speak a word of French. He just stood there as the smile crept off of his face and his brow began to wrinkle; undoubtedly he was most concerned that I was unable to help him with his *souvenirs*, but now was desperately looking for a way to get away from me and this awkward situation and to go back to working the room. And that's when a poilu upstairs in one of the rented rooms provided a distraction. Out of nowhere a shot rang out, which caused everyone in the room who hadn't faced combat before (which was most of them) to duck down or even hit the floor. My American friend went so far as to not only hit the floor but to scoot under my table as well. I for one just froze and listened, which is what long service had taught me to do. There was a commotion upstairs. Some men shouting. A shriek of a woman.

Footsteps up and down the hall. Then, silence. Several officers roused themselves and rushed to the stairs to see what was going on while everyone else more or less tried to both comport themselves and to look concerned. I let my pipe go out in preparation for having to suddenly pack up and leave. Soon what had happened became apparent; a poilu had shot himself in one of the rooms more or less directly above us, and was now lying dead on the floor. I reached in my pocket and took out my little tin of lucifers and relit my pipe.

"Hey, George, get a load of this! Can you believe that one of them just shot themselves upstairs? I told you that they were all scared shitless! Man, I can't wait to get up to where the Germans are and show them how *real* men fight." And so on. And so on. The American officers must have smelt blood and were now instinctively straining at the chain and comparing their penises. How sad and disgusting. Many a night I've struggled with the same hollow, frightening idea: the thought of killing myself, of how easy it would be. Up at the front its as easy as standing up and showing your head over the lip of the trench, that's all it takes to kill yourself. The endless waiting, waiting for someone to kill you. Waiting for someone to maim you, to disfigure you, to dismember you. The waiting begins to gnaw. Begins to gnaw until it reaches the point where you start to look at everything around you and picture yourself killing yourself with it. Your rifle. Your pistol. Your knife. Your shovel. As I sat back and contemplated all of this I gradually became aware of the weight of my pistol in its holster on my side, and some part of me wanted to get up and walk over to the two American braggarts and put it on the table in front of them. But I didn't. I just sipped my whisky and smoked my pipe, and waited for my bath to be ready. In the meantime, I could make out that the innkeeper and his staff were trying to deal with the situation upstairs, and was just able to hear him instructing someone to bring the body down the back stairs and not through the dining room—all in French, of course. How thoughtful.

By now, the mood began to restore itself in the room. Someone cranked the gramophone back to life while another popped the cork on a bottle of champagne. All this merriment was starting to grate on me though. As far as I saw it not too many men in this room had much to celebrate, other than perhaps the chance to fuck a bunch of French whores behind their wives' backs and get away with it. But then again, I've seen the elephant plenty and I didn't feel like I had much to celebrate either. I just earned some leave and was trying to relax. That's all. As I took my last sip of my whiskey drink I began to wonder whether or not I should just forget about the bath and get up and leave. I actually began to gather myself up but when I went to stand I found that the drink had been a little stronger than I had thought, or that perhaps the drink mixed with some strong tobacco from my pipe was proving to be a powerful combination. In either case, my legs were feeling rather spent at the moment, and so on second thought I decided to sit back down. And to not think about anything in particular. When will the bath be ready? I suppose the cleaning up of a suicide takes time, especially given that one cannot simply pitch the body out the front window like you would over the parapet. Though for the moment the idea amused me: what if the snake of an innkeeper simply decided to open a second story window and pitch the late poilu's body out into the street? I suppose that would be bad for business, but just the same the idea seemed fascinating to me at the moment. As this inner debate played on in my head I saw to my delight/dismay that the innkeeper was on his way over to me, and that he had a rather battered silver tray in his hands and a dirty towel draped over his arm. "Monsieur, I would like to apologize for the delay in setting your bath. It has been a busy day around here but I assure you that one will be ready for you in just a little while longer. In the meantime, please accept a small glass of champagne from me as a way to make your wait a little more pleasant." Before I could even really respond, he set a third-full glass on the table in front of me and then disappeared back into the smoky crowd. A busy day? Is that what you call the cleaning up of the contents of a man's head that has been spattered all over the floor of your establishment? I chuffed to myself and then downed the glass in one swig, which turned out to probably be the proper course because whatever it was it wasn't French champagne. And just as quickly as I did the ugly face of the innkeeper reappeared before me, beckoning me with a smile to follow him through the crowd and up the stairs. It looks as if my bath is ready after all.

Upon reaching the landing at the top of the stairs (shakily, I may add), I could see that there were two hallways that branched out from here in either direction, and that there was a small table in front of me that was piled with towels. "Okay, Sergent, here is the deal. I gave you a free drink because you sat out a room full of American officers and managed not to give yourself up and cause a scene. Plus you didn't make a commotion when earlier we had our unfortunate incident, which I appreciate."

At 'incident', he looked down the hallway to the right while I suddenly realized that I could still catch a hint of gunpowder in the air. "In any case, you don't have all night here. I'm going to give you an hour which is longer than most guys get, but I'm setting my watch now. Your towel and cake of soap are on the table in front of you, the bathing room is to your left. I'll see you when your hour is up." At that, he turned and went back down the stairs. Taking my hint I wasted no time in picking out my towel from the grim selection and then my obviously used cake of soap from the slimy tin pan next to them. Slinging my bag and once more feeling the whiskey/tobacco/whatever my free drink was in my legs I sauntered down the hall to the left and toward the sounds of water coming from the room at the end.

My first two steps into this room revealed that it was tiled floor to ceiling in smooth, hard clay tiles, which my hobnailed boots made a startling scratching noise upon when stepped on. There were four great clawfoot tubs arranged in a square with long water pipes descending down to each of them individually from the ceiling, and there was a large mirror on a stand in the corner of the room. Coat racks in the other corners served as places to hang one's uniform, a battered old rattan chair served as a dressing seat, and a large canvas mat on the floor was obviously for the boots judging by the layer of mud dried on it. One large window in the center of a side wall frowned grimly into the street below, and emitted a most feeble and grimy light back into the room through its dirty glass. Or was it almost dusk? Perhaps it was dusk, which surprised me since I hadn't felt that I'd been at this 'inn' for that long. There were currently three other men taking baths, though of what nationality they were it was hard to say from their naked appearances. Plus it was too dark in the room to tell from their uniforms hanging on the coat racks. No matter. They paid me no mind as they soaked, each seemingly taking care to not pay his closest neighbor any mind either. It was silent, too, save for the occasional slosh of water or groan of a hot water pipe—and of course the incessant sounds of 'love making' that were coming down the hall from the other direction. Checking the one unoccupied tub I found that the innkeeper, true to his word, had set my bath for me. Which was a relief, since filling a tub of this size would take a goodly majority of my given hour. Finding the water plenty hot, I dropped my slimy cake of soap into the water and then set to preparing myself to follow it. After hanging my tunic, service belt, and kepi on the unoccupied coat rack I sat down and pulled off my boots. Standing again (and swooning a little in the process, what was in that drink?) I completed the undressing process, and for the moment felt compelled to walk over and examine myself in the mirror. I could see the bruises and cuts that were all over my body, and could tell that I had rashes in sensitive areas, but I felt the urge to really see what I looked like and was going to do it, too, but decided against it since it would be a tad improper on account of my guests. Plus the clock was ticking. Walking over to the tub I braced myself and then slipped in.

And almost fainted. It had been quite some time since I had been submerged in hot water, and the experience rather took my breath away. But in a strangely pleasant way. Like perhaps how a proper lady feigns swooning when she is confronted with either extreme joy or adversity. Perhaps I swooned as I slipped into the water. In any case, my eyes almost immediately closed and my head slunk back against the tub wall, and I was out.

Out. Outside. I was outside. "I'm outside!" I could hear them looking for me in the house. "I'm outside!" Oh bother. No one seemed to be able to hear me which is strange, given that the window to the kitchen is open. Oh well, I'm sure someone will come looking for me out here sooner or later. For the time being, my attention turned back to the garden, and more specifically, to the carrots that seem to be struggling this year. I wonder why? Certainly as much care as ever was put into the soil in between the seasons, which can be attested in the strong growth of virtually all the other plantings. And thanks to our neighbor's friendly suggestion in planting sunflowers all along the edge of the garden we have an abundance of bumblebees. Just listen to them hum as they go about their work, moving from flower to flower, and then across to the buds throughout my garden. After inspecting the stunted green shoots of my poor little carrots and seeing no real evidence of insect attack or of soil decay, I decided to sit down on the lawn in the sun and watch to see if any of the bees ever stopped near the carrots or landed on them at all. I was more curious than anything and besides, after so many days of gloomy rain the warm sunshine felt refreshing. Soon I was stretched out on the lawn with my yard hat pulled down over my eyes, listening to the bumblebees go about their work. If I focused on them, the noise of their little wings at work seemed to fill my very ears. The rhythmic thrumming they made as they passed through the air seemed to grow louder with every passing minute, and as I lay motionless I began to wonder how long I'd have to lay there before one actually landed on me.

And then it was night.

The Imperial German government began the use of airships, or Zeppelins, for strategic bombing of both military and civilian targets by the beginning of the second year of the war. Seen as an act of desperation or malice by many, these bombing raids would eventually occur from Edinburgh to Naples and claim the lives of hundreds, if not thousands of people, mostly civilians. Reims had been the target of German artillery before but this was the first attack by airship. Coming as it did just as night fell it caught the town completely by surprise, and consequently the loss of life was comparatively heavy. Sergent Cloutier's body was never fully recovered and his identification disks were lost, and as a result he was listed as 'missing' officially in the army's register. For their part, the American government was outraged by the attack and the subsequent loss of American lives, and viewed the attack as an act cowardice. They even considered writing a letter to the Kaiser telling him so.

# Chapter Sixteen
# Les Allemands

It was the train whistle that did it. I apparently could sleep through the train coming to a hissing, grinding stop, and sleep through the noise of dozens of sleepy German soldiers rising to their feet and clamoring for the exits. It was the whistle that caused me to jerk awake and gape at my surroundings as my eyes squinted in the dusty sunlight. We were back in France, back in the war zone almost in fact, and it was time to go. "Lars, Lars, wake up. We need to grab our gear and get off the train." Rolf was already awake and was standing in front of his seat with a worried look on his face as he fidgeted with the cord of his sea bag. Lars was still sound asleep, his body undoubtedly worn down by this past week and now trying desperately to heal itself. No matter, he'd need to get up if we were to make it off this train before the goons swept through. "Lars! Wake up! The train has stopped and everyone is getting off. Remember our red stamps, we need to go." He of course heard me; a wry grin slowly spread across his face as he stretched and yawned like an old ally cat.

"Chicken shit. Are you scared of the Feldgendarmerie already? I'm sure that they won't shoot us while we're still on their train." And with that he was up, and soon we were heading out the door of our train car with our bags over our shoulders and a heaviness in our hearts. None of us three, and no one on that train, wanted to go back to the front.

Yet back we went. The journey getting there was not unlike our return from the field hospital after we were wounded. We travelled in lorries that slowly and laboriously trundled us through a green countryside that gradually gave way to a barren wasteland that reeked of chemicals and decomposition. The odor was actually so strong in fact that it was making me nauseous, which at this particular junction was a sort of boon since we hadn't eaten anything since before getting on the train in Metz and I was actually feeling quite hungry up until this point. We actually stopped far short of the actual 'front' however, and were told that in order to conserve fuel all returning front line soldiers were now required to march the last few kilometers in. Which was just the same, as rumor had it that the French and English had shot down most of our aero planes, leaving us only with Zeppelins in which to bomb them back with at night. Any lorry loaded to the gills with soldiers that came too close to the trenches now could just as easily as not find itself all shot to pieces by a low-flying aero plane, which obviously after surviving all that we had endured would be an inglorious way to die. Besides, I'm sure the German army would be hard pressed to lose the lorries at this stage in the game. As we filed off into the muddy fields all around us was a familiar scene: Files of men milling around with their gear while NCOs of every stripe herded little groups together and then headed off with them toward the trench system over the horizon. It was at this juncture that it dawned on me that we had no real instructions on how to find our way back to our unit or section. I knew that Sergeant Pangloss would not be coming for us, or would he be? The idea was ridiculous yet not entirely out of keeping with his character. Looking around I was at a loss and for the moment we three just stood still and took it all in, and perhaps quietly scanned the crowd for a sign of Pangloss. Then I remembered it; our unit number! It was sewn onto the epaulettes of our field tunics. I laughed aloud as I tapped Lars on the arm and then pointed to the red '2' that we all three had emblazoned across our shoulders. He just laughed and rolled his eyes, and even Rolf realized that apparently a week away from the army was all it took to get us to forget how to be soldiers. We immediately picked up our bags and set out in search for anyone else with the same unit markings, and it wasn't long before we found ourselves in a line with other lowing cattle of the same brand. Once enough were assembled we were off, following an Unteroffizer who lead us at a brisk pace back to our place in the line. There was the rumble of artillery off in the distance, and smoke hung on the horizon.

And almost immediately I started feeling afraid. I felt immeasurably small, like an insignificant speck of an insect on a great linen sheet. I felt naked. I felt dead. I couldn't feel the ground. Don't panic. Why panic? Why panic indeed? Breathe…I tried to straighten up and crack my neck, and when I looked over at Lars he was positively green. I didn't know if he had already vomited but he certainly looked as if he could at any moment. Rolf of all people was the one to break the unbearable silence. "It stinks here. And I'm hungry. But it stinks too much." Without even thinking about it I burst out in nervous laughter, only to then shush myself like a nun before anyone could notice. What was wrong with us? We were starting to enter the trench system now, which caused my skin to absolutely crawl to the point that I began to scratch at my arms as we marched along. I had to keep telling myself that there was no possible way for me to have gotten lice again that quickly but all the same it felt like I was swarming with them. All of us in the line began to bob our heads up and down as the once-distant rumbles of artillery began to sound uncomfortably close, and I began to wonder when we would be reequipped with helmets and other proper gear. I'm sure that everyone else was feeling the same, too, as several frontschwein in front of me began to nervously put their hands on top of their heads every time that there was a rumble close enough to be felt. All of a sudden our little line stopped, which gave me the opportunity to gather myself. We were in a communication trench still: There weren't any sand bags across the top nor any strands of wire or other defensive measures. Plus there was no firestep. Other than that, I of course had no idea where we were. As the walls of the trench rose higher than a man on either side of us there was only the old familiar narrow view of the sky above, and it was gray and cloud scudded at the moment. I at least felt better, or at least felt better than I did just a few moments before and my breathing seemed to have returned to normal. Lars was still looking pretty bad, however. "You okay? I wish they'd hurry up and get it over with, I'm ready to get settled in and get something to eat. What about you?" Lars just stared ahead at the file of men in front of us—yet he didn't seem to be looking at them. He looked as if he was staring out into the ocean from the deck of a ship.

"Hey, Lars. You okay?" Suddenly he shook his head and then turned to look at me with the most feral look in his eyes.

"If they want to kill us, why don't they just do it? Why don't they just do it then, huh? Why bother with all this? Huh? Why?" His voice had risen to almost a shout, and his fists were balled like he was ready for a fight. "Who, the French? Of course they want to kill us Lars! I'm sure that no one's feelings toward one another have changed in the week that we were gone."

And with that, I went to slap him on the back as a way to punctuate what I thought was a humorous statement. Except when I went to hit his shoulder he slapped my arm away and recoiled in terror. "No! No! Not the French! The German people! The German people want us dead! Haha!" He was going mad before my very eyes, and I needed to do something quick before a stalking unteroffizer came pushing his way down the line to beat some sense into my friend—or worse.

"Hey, does anyone have a cigarette? A sip of booze? I've got cash right here in my hand." A murmur travelled up the line and back, and before long a stone-faced frontschwein that I had never seen before pushed his way back through the line and up to my sad little scene. "Your friend's a pussy, huh? Here, give him a sip of my canteen, its brandy." With the word 'brandy', Lars quieted up and gladly look the battered canteen and drew a healthy swing from it before handing it back. Without saying a word I put a crumpled papiermark in the soldier's hand, which neither of us looked at since the denomination was really irrelevant. At that he smiled, tucked three cigarettes into the breast pocket of my tunic and then was off back to the place in the line from whence he came. All I could think to say was 'better?' as I turned to Lars with a mixed look of pity and astonishment on my face. "Sure. Why wouldn't I be better? But better than what? Haha!" Better than what. How clever.

Just then, another jostling movement comes down the line and we are off again, only now I can hear voices up ahead. As it turned out we were now being fed into the front-line section proper—though now the 'front' line is really at least four trenches deep. Our pace now was slow, as each soldier was asked to identify himself before an Unteroffizer who would then presumably direct him toward the section of the trench that he originally came from. By now, I was fully expecting to come face to face with Sergeant Pangloss when I turned the corner and was extremely disappointed when I wasn't. Instead I was met by a Sergeant whom I've never seen, and who couldn't have put less effort into his 'examination' of the returning squad of soldiers. As I approached he simply asked to see my identification disk, then glanced at a battered bundle of paperwork, and then finally mumbled something to the effect that I needed to proceed to the left and follow markers until I regained our section of the trench. Which was all fine and good I suppose, but in reality just sent us wandering toward the enemy without any field gear on while being technically in the front-line sector and therefore vulnerable to attack. I was going to bring these concerns and more up to him but he was finished with me before I could and had moved onto the next file already. Which of course was Rolf, followed by Lars. It was refreshing at least to see that he had told them the same thing that he had told me, which meant that he either *did* know where we all needed to go or at least was getting us all lost in the same way. Both Rolf and Lars looked at me as if I was now the defacto leader of our merry little band, and so with a chortle and a shrug of my shoulders that said among other things 'fine' we started off in the direction that we were more or less directed to go. We went left, went about 100 meters, and then saw a sign that directed us to turn left again, and after what seemed like only a few hundred meters more we were back in the war. Voices up ahead. Voices, shouting, jostling of equipment. All three of us were bent so far over by now that I had to croon my neck to keep looking where we were going. Suddenly a machine gun roared to life somewhere up ahead and all three of us simply dropped as if it was us that had been hit with the first burst. How loud it seemed! Its rhythmic rattling 'rat-tat-tat-tat-tat-tat' sounded like someone was beating me over the head with a ballpeen hammer while I was wearing a tin helmet. It was firing in bursts, followed by the shouting of men that due to either distance or my ringing ears was at the moment unintelligible. I shot a glance to Lars, who was frozen with his mouth agape as he stared at the puddle of mud that he was crouching in. "Lars! Lars! It's okay! That's our gun, its shooting at the French, not us! It's as if it is covering for us so that we can make it back to our section—we couldn't be safer!" Which I knew was bullshit since if anything machine guns attract other machine guns, as well as trench mortars and heavy artillery. But no matter, my words seemed to have registered on Lars (and Rolf for that matter, since he was now upright and tugging at my tunic as if to say that he was ready to proceed) since he now was at least able to look at me and eventually to nod his approval. Now if only there was someone to help calm *my* nerves and steady *me* onward…

The machine gun team that was somewhere up ahead must have been well supplied, because it more or less kept right on firing as we advanced ever so cautiously toward it. Finally the noise was almost unbearable as the trench we were in opened up a little to the right to reveal the source of all the noise and anxiety. Here before us was a full MG08 crew hard at work. Their machine was well dug in behind a wall that included sniper shields and sandbags and even had a duckboarded platform from which to operate from. The gunner sat perched behind the piece as he pressed the paddles and fired through an opening in the wall that looked out into no-man's land. Except that the weapon was up on some sort of sled and was angled back at a surprising angle—the gunner would only be able to see sky if he were even looking—which he wasn't! He was just banging away merrily as his crew busied themselves around him, some feeding ammo belts, others topping off the water cans, while others still either oiled the machine or carried boxes of ammo up from somewhere around the corner. How bizarre! They immediately reminded me of the cuckoo clock that my grandparents had on the wall of their house when I was a small boy. When it struck the hour, a wonderful little pageant of small wooden figures would appear from doors in the base of it. They would slowly rotate and perform little tasks like chop wood or carry water while the bells would toll through the given hour. The figures would just carry on with their duties, never paying any mind to each other or to anything else for that matter. They would just keep on until it was time for them to stop and then they would retreat back into the little wooden doors from whence they came. That's what this little machine gun crew looked like to me: like a cuckoo clock that was striking a very long hour as the little figures of the team went about their individual business without paying mind to anything else. That is, all the members of the team but one. There was one lone soldier here who did not belong and who didn't seem to have a job on the machine gun crew. As we picked ourselves up to start moving again we encountered him. He was stationed some distance behind the gun and was presently blocking our way in the trench that we wanted to head down. He was on his knees before a large metal pail and was surrounded by shell casings, while each burst of the gun deposited more around him. Sometimes they would even land on top of him, which seemed to injure him all out of proportion to what hurt was actually being inflicted. He was frantically scooping up the casings with both his hands and then dropping them into his bucket—except his bucket had long since overflowed. In fact, it was practically buried within a mound of casings that had overflowed around it. Yet this soldier kept right on scooping up casings and depositing them into his bucket. As we drew closer I could now see that he was frantic, more than frantic actually. He was mad. His face was streaked with tears and contorted with pain as he repeatedly grabbed handfuls of casings, only to have them tumble back down the mound that grew out of his bucket and over its sides. "The empty shells won't fit in my bucket! The empty shells won't fit in my bucket! The empty shells won't fit in my bucket! Help! Heeeelp!" He was shrieking like a madman at us, with bloodshot eyes that were so wide that the seemed like they would pop right out of his head.

"Help help! The empty shells won't fit in my bucket!" No one on the machine gun team was paying him any mind. No one. I looked at my two companions who were in turn staring at this wreck of a man. Lars seemed to be amused, and seemed to me to be working on the right words in his head for a stupendous insult to lob at this poor fellow. Which I found to be rather cruel, given that he had himself already had a miniature breakdown upon entering the trench system. Rolf on the other hand had a look of absolute pity written across his face. So much so in fact that I saw tears were beginning to flow gently down his cheeks as he contemplated the broken soul before him crouched in the mud. "The empty shells won't fit in my bucket! Help!" It was getting to be time to go. We needed to keep moving, and further I didn't want to give Lars a chance to be cruel. I gave the two of them a nod and picked up my bag in preparation of wading through the brass and over this roadblock, but before I could start Rolf beat me to it. He stepped in front of me, bent down slowly and picked up one solitary 8mm brass shell casing. Holding it before his face he studied it, as if he were trying to discover some hidden meaning within its design. He then took a slow and deliberate step toward the broken man, and making sure that he saw, balanced it ever so gingerly on the mound in his bucket in such a way as to not immediately come tumbling back out. At that, the broken man stopped as if this was the one casing he had been looking for, and he bowed his head and began to sob. The three of us stepped over him softly and tried to disturb his little world as little as possible as we pressed on with our journey toward whatever else waited for us up ahead. And Lars said nothing.

As we plodded foreword the signs of life that one could come to expect in a trench began to appear around us: Shell casings, broken bits of detritus, foul-smelling puddles of muck, and disheveled strands of barbed wire, while all the while the sounds of the gun team behind us began to be drowned out by the sounds of war that slowly enveloped us. Soon we turned another corner and we were there. Here before us was a stretch of the line full of soldiers alternately milling about and manning the parapet. Those that manned the firestep gazed out into the nothing that was the landscape between the lines, which gave the impression that they were ready for anything when in fact there was nothing to see and everyone knew it. We were forced to squeeze past dozens of men and in the process we got our uniforms and our seabags all muddy while the men around us jeered and catcalled at us out of jealousy at us returning from leave. It wasn't long before it looked like we had never left, yet I took care to not let the mud get on my jagdnicker which was still suspended proudly from my belt and which had caught the eye of several of the fresh faces as we pushed past. "Do you have any idea where we are going? Can you see anything up ahead? I don't recognize any of this..." As Lars was carrying on about us being lost it dawned on me: *I Have* been here before. That's right! The machine gun nest was where the sniper was set up when we came back from the hospital! I'm sure of it! That would mean...that would mean that among other things we were close to our dugout if it still existed. It would also mean that just a week ago a man was being employed to methodically pick off the Frenchmen in front of us one by one, and now, that method being deemed unsatisfactory, he has been replaced by a team of automatons and their aimlessly clattering mechanical reaper. At the moment, I didn't have time to really analyze just exactly what that meant, because presently I came face to face with the NCO on duty. "Who are you? Are you supposed to be here? Oh wait, 2nd Bavarian Infantry. Okay. So who are you?" Just then a surly looking Sergeant walked up which caused all four of us to stiffly stand at attention. He had a pad of paper in his hand, and said nothing as he reached out and flipped up my identification disk that was hanging around my neck to check my name against his paperwork. After a moment, he grunted with approval and let my disk fall back to my chest, and only paused for a moment to glance at my Iron Cross before shoving past me to inspect my two companions likewise. After giving the two of them a onceover (I admit I was worried that Lars' name would come up for 'special treatment' on the Sergeant's list), he addressed the three of us brusquely. "Congratulations. You three have managed to find your way back home after a week of whoring and drinking. The Kaiser would be proud of your dedication! Sergeant Pangloss usually oversees this stretch of the line but he is currently not on duty. No matter. Your trunks are all still where you have left them, though other men currently are occupying your bunks. Your leave is over, and you are now out of uniform. See to this immediately! I expect to see the three of you at your posts in five minutes." *Willkommen zuhause* indeed.

# Chapter Seventeen
# Les Allemands reprise

It felt surreal to change into my uniform in front of another man whom I didn't know and who was currently sleeping in what used to be at one point my bunk. But what made it my bunk? Because I slept in it before? What really *did* I own here besides the clothing I had on and my trunk of belongings? And then I thought—*does the army own my clothes?* I had to laugh to myself when I pictured receiving an invoice for the uniform that got ruined during the bombardment I survived. Anyhow, whimsy aside I certainly felt not quite myself as I laboriously changed into my drab and threadbare front-line uniform. Once I was done, it was time for the helmet. *My* helmet of course was lost during the aforementioned bombardment, but the army in its generosity had seen fit to replace it. What was *now* my helmet was different that the one I had before: aside from not having my name carefully written in it there were several immediately apparent differences from the one I used to know and love. For one, the liner to this one was very uncomfortable. Gone were the soft little tanned leather pouches full of padding; in their place was a spartan webbing of aluminum and junk leather that pinched my skin and pulled my hair whenever I turned my head. The chinstrap was different too, and was mounted too far up into the webbing for my liking and seemed to get caught and tangled with my uniform collar too easily. Also, and even more obvious, was the ridiculous paint pattern that was clumsily applied over the entire exterior. My old helmet was a dark gray: This new one was mottled with patches of ochre, dark green, and brown, with black lines separating the patches of color. How ugly! I felt like a clown when I put it on. And I also felt tired. It was *so* heavy. I don't remember my old helmet feeling so heavy. Or so cold. Now that I was almost done and ready to face the day I carefully placed my Iron Cross into my mother's handkerchief, but when I got up to leave I made the split-second decision to wear my jagdnicker with my field uniform for the first time. I don't know why, either. I would already be carrying a club which was standard procedure up here, and of course I'd have a rifle if I needed it, but for some reason I felt safer with the little knife on. Or maybe I just liked the attention it got. In any case, I made sure to move the makeshift sheath around to my front right side of my belt so that everyone could see it—and so it could be accessed quickly if needs be. Now to go find where those other two ended up, since for some reason Lars chose to follow Rolf into his old spot instead of come back to ours.

Stepping back out into the muck of the line I glanced around for any familiar faces and sadly saw none. What happened up here while we were gone? Everyone looked younger than me, which wasn't saying much. Gone too were the Unteroffizer and Sergeant that greeted us upon our arrival which I suppose wasn't altogether strange, since NCOs didn't need to babysit front line troops. Who I'd really like to see was Pangloss though, so that I could let him know that we were back and in one piece. Comporting myself I set off to see what if anything was going on, all the while keeping an eye out for my companions. I could hear the MG08 team clattering away off to my right again. Don't they know it's dangerous to bang away like that? The French are surely to respond with mortar fire or something similar. Yet no one around me seemed to pay any mind, and of course I didn't want to give the impression that I was jumpy. So I just casually walked the opposite direction from which the fire was coming from until I turned the nearest traverse in the trench line—and that's when I ran into my boys.

"Lars! Why, you look like you've lost some weight! Your trousers look baggy enough to fall right off!"

"Shut up, Kurt, these aren't my trousers. I lost all of my clothes one night in Metz and so I had to borrow these before we left." My god. Where did Lars 'borrow' those pants from I wonder. "Well, I guess you don't look a whole lot worse than some of the guys walking around here. Do you need anything? Do you have a shirt on under that tunic?" I winked at Lars when I said that, half expecting him to open his tunic to show off his bare chest. But he just furrowed his brow at me and snorted a little, and then hiked up his trousers by the belt as they started to slip down over his ass. Meanwhile little Rolf poked his head around the corner which coming as it did at a somewhat comically timed moment made me laugh aloud, which seemed to hurt his feelings. "What's funny? Nothing's funny." His injuries always made him deliver his lines in staccato, which was funny in itself.

"Nothing! Nothing at all. You just startled me. Nice helmet, by the way." Poor Rolf. He was so tall and skinny to begin with, and now the helmet he was given looked to be three sizes too big. Between the helmet being so big and its pied paint job he looked like a giant mushroom, the likes of which I'd seen growing in the forest as a boy. "You look great." With that, he straightened up and thrust his chin toward the French, and then the three of us set off for what would be our war today.

And a quiet war it was for the time being. I had thought for sure that the reckless machine gun team down at the end of our line would have drawn some kind of reprisal from our neighbors across the way, but so far no sally of any sort had been sent back to us. Had we all grown so apathetic? These thoughts and more roamed around my head as we shimmied down our trenchline to a section that opened up to a firestep, and that had a few frontschwein milling about smoking cigarettes in it. "Hallo! You guys all new? Any of you seen Pangloss lately? What about that big asshole Jürgen?" My words seemed to fall on deaf ears. They reacted to me as if they didn't speak German, as if they were French farmers or something. I looked at Lars and he just shrugged his shoulders.

"Hey, you guys know who I'm talking about? Pangloss?" As they stood and stared at me a different Unteroffizer (whom I also didn't know) entered the firestepped section from the other direction. "You won't get much out of these men here, they're all Polish POW's who have signed allegiance to the Kaiser to get out of rotting in a cell or building a railroad. I guess they're from Galicia, wherever that is."

He then turned to the POW's and pointed to his Unteroffizer's collar lace, which they all then saluted sharply. "Ha! They think I'm an Oberst or something. God help us if the French ever attack this section of the front again."

And with that he was off, squeezing past us as he whistled to himself. The three of us just stared at each other before slowly turning our gaze back over to our Polish comrades. I couldn't tell if I felt pity for them, or if I was angry for us. Was there no one left in Germany to fight this war? How could they fight for us if they couldn't even take commands? As my mind drifted off in angry thought Lars took upon himself to walk over and try to see if any of them had anything to drink. This left Rolf and I standing there, watching the most pitiful pantomime unfold as Lars tried in vain to act out his desires to these poor unfortunate souls. For their part, they seemed to be really trying hard to accommodate him, one of them even going so far as to repeatedly offer Lars his canteen. So close.

"Where's Galicia?" I smiled as I turned toward Rolf, his questions never failing to elicit the feeling of childhood innocence from me. "Somewhere between Germany and Russia, I think. Maybe where Poland used to be?" Poland used to be. Those words echoed in my mind as I thought about what would happen to France when she finally lost the war. Or us. Just then Lars came trudging back over to us with a disgusted look on his face. Apparently it was harder to act out 'Schnapps' than he thought it would be.

"Don't you think it's strange that no one knows who Pangloss is? I wonder if he's been transferred out to another sector."

All I could think about now was checking in with him. I bet he'd know where Galicia was. "I think this whole damn operation is strange! Our whole trench is full of polackes and yet not one single one of them have anything to drink. You know those dirty drunks have a bottle stashed away!" At that Lars turned over his shoulder as if to direct his angry words back at the group of POWs, who only smiled and waved back at him in blissful innocence. For my part, I was a little taken aback by Lars' anger at other's drunkenness, though at the moment the group of soldiers seemed perfectly sober despite all I'd heard about Polish drinking habits. I also was not a little concerned that Lars seemed to 'need' a drink so badly, given that not long ago that helpful frontschwein had sold us some brandy to calm his nerves. In any case, it looked as if no one here would be able to help him and so we prepared to press on.

But we didn't get far. "You three, wait right there. Where are you stationed? I have a post for you." The voice of the random Unteroffizer that we had just encountered came floating back to us from whence he had gone, causing us all to freeze as if we had just been caught doing something wrong. Just then he came striding around the corner with a determined look on his face. As he approached us we stiffened up and stood at attention. "You three seem to have nothing to do, which is both suspicious and unsatisfactory. You will follow me now as I have an important posting for you. We are expecting an arrival and you will be there to greet it." His words sunk like a stone from my head to my toes. What on earth could he be talking about? Certainly not an attack: the three of us wouldn't be nearly enough to hold back even the smallest of raids. Glancing at Lars I saw that he was on the verge of fainting, and so I tried to assure him with my eyes as we were being led away toward the direction in which this NCO first came from. Brave little Rolf to his credit actually opened the flaps of his ammo pouches on his webbing to check that he had ammo for his rifle before winking at me and falling in behind. Which at the moment it might've actually been better for him to be in the lead.

So off we went, the three of us trailing behind this skinny little Unteroffizer whom we didn't know, toward we didn't know where to, to do we didn't know what: which really could summarize our entire experience in the army up to this point. Just follow. Keep moving. Don't ask questions. Don't fall behind. Yet at the moment I was beginning to realize that perhaps we were getting worked up for nothing. Presently we came to the intersection of two trench lines, which created a small open space that was partially covered over with some type of netting that had sticks and debris woven into it. As we entered this partial clearing the Unteroffizer paused and checked his surroundings before beckoning us to form a file in front of him. "Here, this is your post for the morning. Cold rations are scheduled to be delivered within the hour, you three will take over the delivery to our stretch of the line. Upon receipt of our rations from the ration team, you will bring them back to the firestep where we first met for distribution. I expect the rations to arrive in their entirety, as the army will not tolerate any skimming or theft. You will be very sorry if you test my words! That is all." And with that we three stood sharply at attention as he turned and headed off toward the direction we had just come from. Glancing at Lars I was expecting to see a look of relief written all over his face, yet he was wearing a scowl that would have been more appropriate had be just been handed shovels and told to dig a latrine.

"That fucking does it! So not only do we suddenly have hordes of polackes in our army but now us good German boys get to play waiter and hand deliver their rations up to them while they stand around and smoke cigarettes and sip schnapps all day? This is bullshit!"

He subsequently kicked at a random piece of broken wood that looked dangerously like a French grenade handle and then sat down cross-legged in the mud, his tantrum apparently over. "I thought the Polish soldiers didn't have any schnapps." Rolf's innocence shone through like a beacon, causing me to have to stifle a laugh as I watched his words fall on Lars as he sat there like rain on a toadstool.

"Fuck you, Rolf. Don't lecture me about anything." Oh this was going to be a long hour.

A long, strange hour. As we three settled down and tried to make ourselves as comfortable as possible we of course began to become more in tune with our surroundings. Well, I did anyway, and presumably Rolf did as well. His tantrum over for the moment Lars chose to find a patch of ground that was less rotten than the rest and quickly drop off to sleep. Which was a blessing and a curse, since I was starting to feel really alone on this battlefield. Presently the rumble of artillery could be made out in the distance: Then the occasional rattle of a machine gun or a crack of a rifle. All very far away. Or maybe not. Being below ground played tricks on your hearing while at the same time amplified vibrations through the earth. Sometimes even the direction of the wind could play tricks on your hearing as it helped project sounds further than they otherwise might have travelled on their own. And right now either due to the wind or my nerves or a combination of the two the war sounded like it was getting closer as the minutes ticked by. I glanced over at Rolf who at the moment had his ear cocked toward the general direction of the French as if he were straining to hear something in particular, and as I studied him standing there I suddenly realized that we three were practically unarmed. Sure, I mean, we had our three rifles with us and I for one knew that my ammo pouches were full, but that was essentially it. It was standard procedure to use grenades to repel an attack on an individual basis while the machine gunners handled the rest, yet here we three stood (two really, Lars was fast asleep) without any real means of defending this trench if it were to come under attack. What a stupid little Unteroffizer to lead us out here like this, to lead us out without at least a few sandbags full of grenades. Pangloss would have never done that.

Straitening up and clearing my throat I tried to exude an air of bravado as I strolled over to the edge of the traverse and pretended to casually glance around the corner. The coast was of course clear, and so I stepped out and shifted my rifle to my other shoulder before turning back around and strolling a few paces the other way. Rolf took the hint, and was soon standing like a sentry, occasionally peering ahead or behind as if there was anything to see. Sometimes we'd even catch each other's glances and when we did we would both smile and give a sort of nod as if to say "everything's okay, all clear."

Which was nonsense since there was no way of knowing if everything was *really* okay. Which I guess began to weigh on my nerves as I paced about looking for action. Maybe I was just wearing myself out like this. Maybe it *would* be better to rest and save my strength for the off chance that someone unwanted would hop over the parapet and need to be dealt with. Maybe I should lie down. Maybe Lars has the right idea. After a few more minutes of my internal struggle playing out, I found that my legs no longer wanted to pace back and forth, and so without further ado I plopped down next to Lars in the mud and started glancing around for ways to make myself more comfortable. Rolf came over, and smiling, simply said, "You rest, I'll keep watch," which was as sweet a statement as any soldier could make to another.

"Cigarette?" Of course—I still had the three cigarettes that I got earlier in my tunic pocket, to which I gladly gave him one.

"Do you have matches?" He just smiled at me and nodded, and with that my helmet was off, and somehow without giving it too much thought I was curled up next to Lars and very rapidly drifting off to sleep.

Yet as I did so my tired mind began to wander. If our army is full of Polish refugees now, who is fighting for the French? We must have killed most of the able-bodied Frenchmen by now, who was hiding in the trenches across the way? Russians? Or worse—Cossacks? Chinamen? Maybe tribesmen from Africa? Hmm, Africa. I could see them all in my mind, swarming about their trenches like scurrying little rats, each a different color and making different little noises. This wasn't so bad, all these colorful little rats. And there we all are, standing proud and strong in our trenches, pointing and laughing at the little creatures across the way. Look at them scurry! Some of our men have begun to take pot shots at them now—see how they run! Oh the war won't last much longer, all their rats are running away! Running away. Running away...half asleep I rolled onto my right side which put me facing Lars, who was fast asleep on his back. Without trying my head rested against his shoulder, then slumped down onto his chest. Soon his breathing was all I could hear in my lucidly dreaming mind, yet I could sense that something wasn't quite right. It was the rats that I could hear breathing...breathing all at once in their deep holes across the way. Breathing all at once as if they were gathering their strength for something big. Something monumental. Nobody else seemed to be able to hear them breathing, but I could. I knew what they were up to, and I was ready. No multi-colored and mixed-up mass of divergent rats was going to get a jump on me. No sir. I was ready, I could hear them. Even if no one else could. Breathing. Breathing all as one. Clever rats. But wait! No! Can it be? It can't be. There are blue helmets rising up from under the rats! I'm sure of it! Blue helmets like the French soldiers wear, oh can you see them? Does no one else see them? There are soldiers hidden in the rats! Why does no one see? I see them, I see them! Let them come! I am ready! And come they are. Slowly I can see them oozing their way out of their trenches, hidden by the swarming mass of squealing rats. Crawling on their stomachs as to not be seen by careful eyes. But I see them! I have careful eyes! No one's eyes are as careful as mine, and I am ready. Too far away still, too far away. Let them come closer so that you can shoot them. Kill them. Yes. Closer. On they come, slithering under their rats on their bellies like snakes. I won't let them in. I won't let them in! I will kill them all, even if no one else sees them. I have careful eyes. Look! One peers up over the rats. Black as the ace of spades he is. Black as night. A Senegalese! Ho! How fierce he is—he has a giant knife in his hands! Does no one see? I will shoot him. Shoot him dead before my trench. But oh no! He's spotted me and gone back down in his rats. A Senegalese! They must be everywhere! How horrible! No one wanted to fight a Senegalese. So big, so strong. With horrible knives. Damn the French for their Senegalese! But I see them, they are too big to hide. Too big and black to hide. Yet they are all hidden. Hidden beneath their rats and coming closer. Does no one else see? No matter, I will shoot them. There! A helmet so very close to me! Let him rise up, up, yes. Rise up and look at me so that I can shoot you. You dirty African savage. Show me your face so that I can shoot it. Oh how the rats churn as he rises, lifting his helmet to look at me. Look at me and…

He has no face!

No face! He has no face! Ah! Ah! Aaaaah! He has no face! He has worms pouring out of his face! Worms and slime! He is rotting before my eyes! No, no, no! He sees me! He's raising his bony arm and pointing with his bony hand that's wrapped around his giant knife. Does no one else see? He's pointing at me! Worms are slithering everywhere!

I must have been thrashing as much as I was screaming when I woke up, because Lars cried out as he was jerked awake and swatted me away as if he was under attack. Rolf came running, too, though I have no way of knowing how far away he was at the time. At any rate, the three of us had varying reactions to what turned out to be my very bad dream. For Lars, he was angry at being awoken so. "Goddammit, Kurt! What the fuck is wrong with you! Jesus Christ are you really going to wake me up like that?"

For me, I was still gripped in horror. "Get them off! Get them off! Get them off! The worms. The Rats! Rolf look out! The rats!" I kept rolling over and over in the fetid mud in the bottom of the trench as I cowered and glanced about wildly for the bogeymen and their rat accomplices that I was certain were to descend upon our trench at any moment. And Rolf? Christ-like compassion. While I was rolling around and Lars was sitting there and cursing me out, Rolf rushed over to my side and knelt down in the mud, resting his hand on my shoulder and holding me still so that I would calm down. He then grabbed my face and turned it toward his, and simply said, "It's okay. It's okay. There's no rats right now." And that was that. Then I was back. Standing up (shakily I must admit, and with a sudden twinge of pain from my wounded knee that seemed to come from nowhere) I sort of tried to brush myself off and gather my senses. And belongings. As I checked all of my pockets and reclosed all of my pouches my right hand slid over to check my knife—and it was gone! As a wave of anxiety swept over my body and I tensed as if I were about to dive manically into searching for it again, Rolf just gently placed his hand on my shoulder to calm me down. "Here it is. Be careful, its sharp." There, sitting handle-out in his outstretched hand was my jagdnicker, muddy but safe. All I could do was flash a nervous smirk as I gently took it from him, wiped it off on my equally muddy trousers, and then carefully slipped it back into its homemade sheath. And Lars did nothing.

"What the fuck is wrong with you? Did something bite your ass while you were asleep?" As I gazed at him, astounded by his callousness, I was mortified to see not Lars' face but the face of my father. I saw the face of my father as he stood in the darkened doorway to my bedroom, door ajar, candle holder in hand, as he peered into the darkness and onto me as I sat with my knees balled up to my chest crying in my bed. I could see my father's face straining in the darkness to find if there was something actually the matter with me. Straining to see if there really was a good reason for him to have had to pull himself away and to have had to come down the hallway and have had to of used a precious lucifer to light a candle to come and check on me. I could see his angry face as he watched me shiver and weep in my bed. I could see his angry face suddenly disappear as he blew out the candle in disgust and slam the door without saying a word. I could see how the darkness enveloped me again, could smell the acrid aroma of the snuffed-out candle, could hear my father's footsteps down the hall and then my parent's bedroom door slam shut, could hear my mother's muffled cries and her struggle in the darkness…the ashen face of stone that I turned toward Lars was apparently enough to scold him into silence. Apparently enough to tell him that he had hurt me. Apparently enough, to say that I'd apparently had enough. I said nothing to him. And he said nothing further. And Rolf cleared his throat. And then there were footsteps from around the corner.

Footsteps, then voices. "Ho, hallo? Hallo?" Rolf was first to jump up, but then froze when he did in sort of a dog-pointing stance, like he had just found a quail and now didn't know what to do with it. We could hear several voices conversing (in German) lowly just around the corner of the traverse. I looked at Lars, who was at the moment staring at the ground as he fumbled with his bayonet that he was clumsily attempting to fix to his Mauser. Great. Realizing that I'd been chosen for leadership yet again I took a deep breath and a step closer to the corner. "Who's there? You are attempting to enter a German frontline trench and I demand you identify yourselves!" My bravado felt pretty good, though at the moment I was half expecting a grenade to come sailing over the top and into our faces. I glanced to my right at Lars who to his credit had now fixed his bayonet and who was now peering in the direction of the voices, and then to my left at Rolf, who looked as if he hadn't moved. "This is a German ration party bringing up cold rations, and you had better *damn* well be our relief." As his words trailed off I became aware of some shuffling and clinking noises that were coming from the other side of the traverse, and realized that the men could very likely be arming themselves for a rush around the corner. I took another deep breath and slowly unsheathed my little jagdnicker and held it upside down in my right hand. Rolf took a step back and put his rifle across his body. Lars almost silently worked the bolt of his rifle to put a round in the chamber. "Of course we're your relief you dumb shit! Now bring the food around the corner so that we can take it from here." Then there was silence for what seemed like an hour. No one moved, and for the moment all I could hear was the far-off rumble of sporadic artillery in the distance. Then it happened. There was a shuffling noise low in the trench, toward the ground. A shuffling noise of something moving. "Look! There!" Something was moving. Lars pointed his rifle at the dark shape that began to emerge from around the corner. "Look!"

A box of biscuits. A box of biscuits was being pushed out into the trench in front of us by the ration party on the other side of the traverse. A fucking box of biscuits. As it scooted out there came the voice from the other side again. "Here, are you happy? Do you want your damn lunch or not?" I spontaneously burst out into laughter at the release of the tension as I slid my knife back into its sheath.

"Alright guys cease fire. Stand down. C'mon let's give them a hand." At that, we all put away our weapons and came forward to fulfill our original mission. Out from around the traverse poked a helmeted head, and then body of a frontschwein who was apparently the soldier I was just chatting with.

"Goddamn you guys are wired tight. What gives? Are you guys new or something?" At that Lars shot this soldier a fiery glance which in the fading light of the afternoon particularly showcased his facial scars.

"Oh, I see. You're just burnouts." I did not want a fist fight over some crackers just then and so yet again had to take the situation in hand.

"All right all right, just give us what you have. We need to get back with this shit before the sun goes down." That seemed to be enough, because in short order the two other soldiers who were with the one I was speaking with quickly piled three crates on top of one another in front of me, followed by a large basket with a hinged lid and two large carboys with wicker covers that were connected by a rope. "Here you assholes go. Enjoy." I just looked at the pile of impedimenta in front of me and then flashed my new acquaintance a parting forearm jerk, to which he in kind sneered at me and then turned around to lead his little squad of boys back to the safety of the rear areas.

"Well that was fun. Goddamn, those guys could've gotten themselves killed back there, right?" Turning to Lars I was half expecting a high-five or some kind of celebratory gesture, or even a verbal response to my bravado, but instead I got an eyeful of the enfeebled addict with his mind racing on to bigger things. He was shaking, either from fear or something worse, as he struggled mightily to put his bayonet back into its frog. "Hey Lars, don't forget that you still have a round in the…" before I could even finish the statement he had tossed the rifle aside and was pushing past me to get to the carboys sitting in the mud of the trench floor. Sighing, I stooped and picked the rifle up and cycled the round back out of the chamber—half out of duty, half out of fear of my own safety. Lars didn't even notice.

"What kind of shit is this? These jugs are full of cold tea! Both of them! The only reason I agreed to go on this mission was to be able to finally get a drink! Dammit!" And so on, and so on. As he was carrying on about how he had been unjustly robbed of his well-deserved afternoon tipple I had to laugh to myself.

"Agreed to go on this mission? Since when are we consulted?" I had had just about enough out of him and besides, this stuff wasn't going to carry itself.

"Alright enough, Lars. I don't know why it's come as a shock to you that we weren't just handed magnums of champagne to go along with our stale bread and rotten meat, but nevertheless it's our job to hump it back to the rest of the guys. So get your shit together and let's move." Boy, I was starting to sound like a real NCO sometimes, and wondered if Pangloss would agree—whenever it was that we finally got to see him again. Lars shot me an ugly look and then slung the disappointing carboys over his shoulders and lifted two of the wooden boxes with a jerk in preparation to go. Rolf then grabbed the third box, which then only left the large basket (which turned out to be only full of stale bread, which was very light) for me. Picking it up I turned to Lars who seemed to have gleaned my intent and was one step ahead of me. "No no, go ahead and carry the bread. I don't want you to strain yourself." I just smiled and shook my head at him as we three picked up (and I picked up Lars' rifle) and started heading back to our line. Lars insisted for some reason on going first, too, and it wasn't long before he was even pulling ahead. I suppose he was trying to show off, but I didn't care. Either did Rolf, who slid up behind me as we walked and spoke for the first time in what seemed like forever. "Sometimes he's an ass, sometimes he's a mule."

Laughing, all I could get out was an 'exactly' as we began our trudge back up to the front line in earnest and the far-off artillery rumbled in the distance.

# Chapter Eighteen
# Les Allemands perdent tout

Hungry soldiers always have the same look on their faces, regardless of what language they speak or rank they hold. And hungry faces are what greeted us as we came back up on our previous position. It was the Polish soldiers that greeted us first, and despite not being able to communicate understood perfectly what we were carrying. Then came the skinny little Unteroffizer that sent us up to get all of this in the first place. "You three are late with our rations! This is unacceptable, I will not tolerate men slacking on their duties. I should strip you of your rations for this offense!" We three just stopped in our tracks at this assault, perhaps as if to say that if we weren't going to get anything to eat then we weren't going to carry it any further. But then it was sweet Rolf of all people who piped up in our defense.

"No. The ration party was late. And then they almost attacked us. And us them. It took time to sort out." As this little exchange was going on and the three of us were standing there with everyone's lunches a gaggle of polish soldiers stood watching with pensive looks on their faces despite not knowing what we were saying—hunger transcends language barriers, and they knew that we had the food.

"Oh, is that so? Ration parties are supposed to announce themselves as such. No one got hurt, I suppose?" With his change in tone came a relaxing of the tension, which gave me the window I was looking for.

"That's right. We were poised to defend our position because they failed to identify themselves properly, and this took time to diffuse before all parties were satisfied. Now, sir, if we could please be directed to where you would like these rations deposited we would be much obliged, as they are heavy." I shot Lars a smirky glance when I said that too, which he pretended not to see.

"Very well. I shall see to it that the party that was sent will be spoken to (I knew he was lying), and in the meantime you may stack the rations in front of my dugout there in order to be distributed." Relieved, we trudged our burden over to where we were directed and then rushed back to our dugouts to grab our eating utensils.

And of course by the time be got back and into line we were close to the end of it. "Bullshit! We had to risk our necks to get the food and then carry it all the way back here and then don't even get to cut in line?" Lars was really feeling miffed at this whole experience, though I bet he'd feel differently if there had been schnapps in those carboys.

"When is the army fair?" Hitting the nail on the head was our sweet little Rolf again, who once again didn't fail to both summarize the situation and garner an ugly face from Lars in response. I was just hungry, and was hopeful that there would be enough of whatever it is that we were given by the time we made it up to our little friend. But judging by the solemn faces of the soldiers retuning back with their plates the fare was not good, which dampened the spirits slightly. In any case, the line was moving, and before long we rounded the corner and could see the food being doled out ahead. And to my disappointment, it was just the little Unteroffizer who was doing the doling. Where was Pangloss? He must have secured himself some leave after he did us the favor, that sly devil.

With our battered plates and cups out, we looked up at our Unteroffizer like urchins as he stood stone-faced before us and reached down into the boxes and basket that we carried up for him. One battered turnip. One moldy hunk of dark bread. One very little piece of very dried out sausage. And one splash of cold tea in our dirty cups. Thank you very much.

"Oh, I'm sorry sir, I ordered the schnapps." Lars was trying to be cute with our new NCO but he wasn't having it.

"Schnapps is for NCO's and officers, frontschwein get tea. Now move along." Miffed but not surprised, move along we did. Back toward the area by our dugout since we assumed that we would be relived of further duties for the day which was typically the case. Yet as we shuffled along past groups of soldiers milling around and eating their rations I could see that something was again wrong with Lars. He kept wincing as we had to squeeze past the others, cowering in some cases even. What gives? I didn't understand what was so frightening about a group of men trying to choke down their rations, but somehow having to bear witness to this was almost too much for him. I was almost starting to wish that somehow he had gotten his wish for a drink as that was probably all that was the matter with him. I didn't even bother to ask, either, but instead just focused on trying not to get mud in my already unpleasant-looking food as we moved along.

But to our dismay, we weren't the only frontschwein thinking of taking in the view for lunch in front of our new digs. There were several soldiers standing or sitting in cutouts in the trench walls eating their plates of food around our dugout, which didn't bother me in the slightest but seemed to almost enrage Lars. He kept glancing around with an almost wild look on his face as his grip on his plate kept getting tighter, and tighter. Rolf just stopped and shot me a look, and some of the other soldiers seemed to notice as well.

"Hey, Lars, calm down. I'm sure that no one wants any more of this food than they've been given. And as for seating, I'm sure that the maître d'ho-tel can find us a table if he looks." To which Lars said nothing. So I just shrugged my shoulders at Rolf and went over and leaned on a dry-looking portion of the trench wall and started to assess my lunch. Rolf came over too and leaned against the wall next to me. Taking his cue, Lars shuffled over and sat down on the cut out in front of us, setting his tin cup full of tea down in the mud next to him. Looking over today's lunch option I could see that things must not have been going well for the commissary department in this grand army of ours; the turnip I was given was so battered that it looked as if it had been used to play a game of bandy with, yet at its core it was hard as a rock, and my bread was very dry with a fine white powdery mold growing on it that was difficult to brush off. As for the hunk of sausage I was given, it was most certainly rancid and had barely any grease left to it, which made me suspect that it was made with a lot of oats (or sawdust) for binding. But I was hungry, and I've eaten worse, so I took a deep breath and tucked in. Tearing a small piece of bread off, I took a bite and looked into the sky. There were black birds circling overhead. Black, far-off birds. I couldn't remember the last time I had seen a bird in the trenches, hell, there weren't any trees around here for miles. Yet there they were, three, or maybe four large black, far-off birds. I wondered if they were crows. Or buzzards, or…

Crunch! What an awful sound! I spun to my left to catch the tail end of Rolf biting into his turnip like an apple. Oh what a spectacle to see him now; poor Rolf, with his poor mauled mouth and stub for a tongue, trying to eat a turnip that was undoubtedly as hard and unforgiving as the one on my plate. He was chewing with his mouth wide open, which, if we were at a dinner table I would reprimand him for. But we weren't. We were standing in shit and eating rotten food in a muddy trench somewhere in France. So I ignored them, the eating sounds he was making, be them ever so foul. Crunnch! He sounded like a horse eating a bushel of carrots. Poor Rolf. Swallowing hard, I was able to get the bread down my throat though a sip of tea would be in order. Balancing my plate in my left hand I reached down and grabbed my tin cup full of tea (and mud flecks) and as I did so my gaze swept casually over Lars. He was sitting in the mud with his knees up to his chest, breathing hard and rocking back and forth. He was mumbling under his breath, too, and was again wincing and cowering at the noises going on around him. Poor bastard. Crunnnch! Poor Rolf, that has to not feel good, biting that turnip like that. And I seemed to remember that he never liked turnips. Crunnnch! I raised my cup to my lips and tried not to think about what I was putting in my mouth. Then I was thrown back. My cup fell from my right hand. My plate fell from my left hand. I felt myself being slammed back up against the trench wall behind me. My plate went crashing to the ground. My cup tumbled away. Lars leapt up before me, hands outstretched. His hands. His hands were in my face. His left hand over my mouth. His hands were all over me.

"What are you doing? What, are, you…" His right hand shoots to my waist. He's grasping me. He's grabbing me. He's hurting me!

"Stop! Let me go! What are you…" Rolf is at my side. He's dropped his food too. He still has turnip in his mouth and cannot cry out. My knife! My knife! My knife! What are you doing?

The sound air makes when it exits a man who's just had a knife plunged into his chest is unique. From the impact of the blade and the force of the arm behind it, the air comes out of the mouth all at once. Sometimes this can be in a yell, or a shout, especially since this entire process usually involves combat. Other times the air can exit like a belch, and can even be comical. Then other times, it can exit like a long hiss, as if passing over clenched teeth and drawn lips. When Lars slammed my father's jagdnicker into Rolf's chest, he did so with all of his weight behind it. He may have even thrown his body forewords as he did so. And when he did so, the air exited Rolf's body with a long, low hiss. Or maybe a hiss mixed with a gasp at the end. But in any case, it all came out. All of the air. I could tell because when you stab a man, if you get all the air to come out of him, he then falls to the ground and perhaps tries to gasp for breath. Or he just dies. In Rolf's case, he just died. As frail as he was, Lars must have put that little knife halfway through him. As Rolf's little body collapsed to trench floor I just stood there for a moment, mouth agape, staring at him. Finally, my gaze lifted to Lars, who was standing there, panting like a dog. Without thinking I lunged at him but as always, he was faster than me. So quick on his feet was Lars, those cat-like reflexes of his. He just moved out of the way, jumped to the right, and as usual I slipped and fell down to the trench floor and onto my knees. Quickly I gathered myself as if to leap back up but before I could, Lars cried out, "Look!"

"Look!" I looked. I looked up to see him, my little bloodied knife in his right hand, nothing in his left, and a small grin across his lips. I looked up to see him smile at me, to look back at me, to look into my eyes. I looked up at him to see his right hand slowly raise up to his throat, to slowly rise up and reach across toward his left ear. I looked up at him to see him draw the blade across his throat, slowly, from left to right. Ear to ear. I looked up to see him falling, falling down onto his knees before me. I looked into his eyes as he landed before me. I looked to see my little knife fall out of his right hand, and to see his head fall foreword, and to see him fall toward me. I looked to see him lying face down in the muck before me, blood streaming from his neck and pooling before me, and could hear voices and footsteps all around. I looked up to see three, or maybe four large black, far-off birds circling, and wondered if they might be buzzards.

*Gott mit Uns. Deutschland uber Alles. Alles Null-acht Funfzehn.*

To be continued.

# Glossary of Terms

*Adrian*—French, or *'M15 Adrian'* was the standard issue steel helmet furnished to France's fighting forces in the First World War beginning roughly in 1915. It was an effective design that was eventually adopted by many other armed forces including Russia, Italy, Belgium, Serbia, and Poland. The *Adrian* helmet continued to serve as the standard issue helmet of the French forces with few modifications up until the eve of the Second World War.

*Albatros D*—German, a family of fighter aircraft produced by the *'Albatros Flugzeugwerke'* company for the German air service during the First World War. There was a total of five models produced, numbered I through V (e.g., D.I, D.II, etc.) over the course of the conflict.

*Alles Null-acht Funfzehn*—German, literally translates to English, "all zero-eight fifteen." This phrase would more commonly be expressed "All is 0-8/15" in reference to the *MG 08/15* heavy machine gun which was the most prevalent model of German machine gun during the First World War. The colloquial phrase came to mean "nothing special, business as usual" in reference to the common sight of the *MG 08/15* machine gun and in a broader sense the conflict itself. *(See MG 08/15)*

*Annamite*—French, in reference to the people of Annam, which at the time of the First World War was a French Protectorate encompassing central Vietnam within French Indochina. Peoples from this region, *Annamites*, were brought to the Western Front during the First World War and used by the French military mainly as construction crews, cooks, drivers, or in any other number of non-military roles.

*Attends ici*—French, translates to English, "Wait here."

*Au Revoir*—French, translates to English, "Goodbye."

*Bandy*—A team winter sport played on ice in which players use long curved sticks to direct a ball into an opponent's net. Similar to ice hockey, *Bandy* was very popular in Western Europe at the time of the First World War.

*Bayer Heroin*—A reference to Heroin produced by the Bayer pharmaceutical company in Elberfeld Germany. Bayer was the first company to synthesize heroin on an industrial scale and therefore was key to its commercialization. *Bayer heroin* was commonly available over the counter in tablet form throughout the western world at the time of the First World War and was not yet considered a narcotic despite its similarities to opium, whose attributes were then already well known.

*Bayou*—French, soldier's slang for a communication trench.

*Bierkrug*—German, literally translates to English, "beer mug."

*Bitte*—German, translates to English, "Please."

*Black Forest*—Is a large forested mountain range in the south-west corner of Germany, located within the state of Baden-Wurttemberg.

*Blotto*—Soldier's slang for drunkenness, also slang for "to soak," or "soaked."

*Boches*—French, soldier's slang for a German soldier or infantryman.

*Camion*—French, translates to English, "truck, or lorry."

*Capitaine*—French, translates to English, "Captain."

*C'est la vie*—French, a common phrase that can be translated to English as "It's life," or "Such is life."

*Chained Dog*—soldier's slang for *Feldgendarmerie* (a type of German military police), which was a direct reference to the distinctive steel gorget worn around the neck as part of the standard field uniform. *(See Feldgendarmerie)*

*Chauchat (Light Machine Gun)*—French, refers to the *"Fusil Mitrailleur Modele 1915 CSRG,"* which was the standard light machine gun of the French armed forces during the First World War beginning in 1916. Chambered in 8 x 50R mm (the same as the *Lebel* rifle) and fed by 20-round curved box magazines, it was of a compact enough design to be carried and employed by a single infantryman, making it an effective close support weapon for advancing infantry as well as a dynamic tool for fluid defense. Despite its somewhat problematic design, the *Chauchat* was the most widely manufactured machine gun of the war and continued to serve with various other nation's armed forces through the Second World War. *(See Lebel)*

*Chopin*—Frederic François Chopin was a Polish composer and pianist of the Romantic era.

*Club, Trench Club*—A generalized term referring to melee weapons of either official or unofficial manufacture which were employed by infantrymen of all belligerent nations during the First World War. These clubs were primarily employed for nighttime raids or in situations of hand-to-hand combat in extremis, and generally consisted of a length of wood or steel that was weighted at one end and may have had spikes or barbs of various design driven into the weighted end for additional effect.

*Coal-Scuttle Helmet*—soldier's slang for the *Stahlhelm* helmet worn by soldiers of the Imperial German Army after 1916. *(See Stahlhelm)*

*Cordite*—Is a type of smokeless propellant that was used extensively during the First World War for projectiles ranging from rifle ammunition to large artillery shells. It remained in service throughout the Second World War as well, and in some instances up until as late as the end of the 20th Century.

*Coutrot*—French, soldier's slang for the "Poignard-Baionnette Lebel M1886/14" issue trench knife, which were manufactured from the stiletto bayonet of the *'M1886 Lebel'* rifle. *(See Lebel)*

*Crown Prince*—Here in reference to His Royal Highness Rupprecht Maria Luitpold Ferdinand, Crown Prince of Bavaria, Duke of Bavaria, of Franconia and in Swabia, Count Palatine of the Rhine. He was both the last heir apparent to the Bavarian throne and a successful field commander of Bavarian forces during the First World War.

*Deutschland Uber Alles*—German, translates to English, "Germany above all." The phrase *Deutschland Uber Alles* had been used in national poetry and song form the mid-19th century, eventually becoming the first lines of the German national anthem in 1922.

*Driving Band*—In reference to an artillery shell, a driving band is a soft metal band made of copper of other gilded metal that is around the base region of the shell. When fired, this band engages the rifling of the cannon barrel and imparts spin to the shell, which both stabilizes it and greatly increases its accuracy. During the First World War it was not uncommon for *driving bands* to be readily found liberally strewn over battlefields, especially given the static nature of the conflict. As such, *driving bands* became favorite souvenirs for soldiers to pick up in order to be made into trinkets, given the malleability of the metals employed.

*Dugout*—A protective hole that was literally 'dug out' of the side of the trench wall in order to provide protection from flying ordinance and debris. A *dugout* could vary from anything as simple as a hole in the dirt for a single man to an elaborate structure designed to house a multitude of soldiers featuring proper floors and roofs and, in some cases, even doors. *(See Stollen)*

*"Escusez-moi. Je suis le lietentant Cloutier. Je te depasse alors bouge ton cul pour que je puisse prendre un verre"*—French, translates to English, "Excuse me. I am Lieutenant Cloutier. I outrank you, so move your ass so I can get a drink."

*Feldgendarmerie*—German, were a type of military police unit fielded by the armed forces of Germany from the early 19<sup>th</sup> Century through the Second World War. *Feldgendarmerie* companies were comprised of combat infantrymen led by *NCOs*, and were used primarily for occupation and policing duties though also could be called upon to combat partisan activities as well. *(See NCO)*

*Feldgrau*—German, was the official color introduced by the Imperial German army to replace the multitude of traditional more brightly-colored uniforms of the 19<sup>th</sup> century. Officially it was of a light grayish-green color, but due to wartime restrictions on dies and paints and the use of recycled fibers during the First World War it could range in color greatly, and came to include hues of brown, dark gray, and dark green as well. *Feldgrau* additionally served as the basic color of the German armed forces' uniforms throughout the Second World War.

*Feldmutze*—German, a soft wool forage cap worn by German soldiers during the First World War in place of their helmets. These caps were typically worn when not engaged in combat-related duties.

*Fire step*—A platform used by soldiers in a trench to literally 'step up' to fire their weapons over the parapet. Typically, the fire step was either carved out of the trench wall itself or constructed out of sandbags or similar materials.

*Flechette*—a pointed steel projectile with some form of a tail assembly for stabilized flight. During the First World War *flechettes* were dropped by aircraft as a form of ground attack, and were most effective when deployed over large formations of troops or more commonly, over lengths of occupied trenches.

*Flying Circus*—soldier's slang for a fighter wing of the German air forces, which at full strength contained four squadrons or *"Jastas."* The term is thought to have originated in reference to Manfred von Richtofen's (the Red Baron's) *"Jasta,"* though the term at times seems to appear to be used more generally. Also, the origin of the term itself is unclear, though references to

Richtofen's red aircraft and garish paint schemes employed by other pilots have been made. *(See Jasta)*

*Forearm Jerk*—An offensive hand gesture that is commonly used throughout Western Europe which can be considered the equivalent of 'flipping the middle finger' in the United States.

*Frontschwein*—German, soldier's slang, literally translates to English, *"front pig,"* which was used as a derogatory term for long-serving soldiers in the front lines.

*Gewehr 98(Rifle)*—German, was the standard infantry rifle of the German armed forces during the First World War. Chambered in *8mm Mauser* (Note: actual cartridge dimensions are 7.92 x 57mm), it was a bolt-action, magazine-fed rifle featuring an internal box magazine capable of holding up to five rounds. Of such a successful design, it served as the basic pattern for bolt-action military rifles for many nations' armed forces through the Second World War. *(See 8mm Mauser)*

*Gott mit Uns*—German, translates to English, "God with us." The phrase *Gott mit Uns* is a common heraldic phrase within Prussia that was adopted by the German military in the latter half of the 19th century, and at the time of the First World War was found stamped or painted onto various components of its military's uniforms such as belt buckles and Prussian *Pickelhaube Wappens*. *(See Pickelhaube, Wappen)*

*Grossvater*—German, translates to English, "grandfather."

*Hallo*—German, translates to English, "Hello, hi."

*Hobnailed Boots*—Boots with hobnails driven into the soles in a pattern to provide grip on muddy surfaces, which were commonly worn by soldiers of all belligerent nations on the Western Front during the First World War.

*Hohenzollern*—Or the *House of Hohenzollern* is a German dynasty of former princes, electors, kings, and emperors that can trace its roots back to the 11th century. Used here in reference to *Kaiser Wilhelm II of the House of Hohenzollern* who was German Emperor during the First World War. (See Kaiser, Crown Prince)

*Horizon Blue*—French, was the official color introduced by the French armed forces to be used for uniforms during the second year of the First World War (1915). This was to replace some of the brighter more traditional colored uniforms that were still being employed at the start of the conflict and that harkened back to the age of Napoleon. *Horizon blue* was used for coloring in trousers, great coats, and as a paint color for *Adrian* helmets, and was of a bluish-gray hue. *(See Adrian)*

*Iron Cross*—German, the '*Iron Cross Medal*' was a medal first adopted by the Kingdom of Prussia in 1813 during the Napoleonic Wars, was later used by Imperial Germany until 1918, and then later still with modification by Nazi Germany until 1945. During the First World War it was awarded in three classes; Second Class, First Class, and Grand Cross of the Iron Cross, and can be recognized by its distinctive *cross pattee* of the Teutonic Knights design.

*Iron Cross, Second Class*—(See Iron Cross)

*Jagdnicker*—German, *jagdnicker* loosely translates to "hunting knife," or "knife used to sever the nicker (nodder)" and is a traditional hunting knife carried by German and Austrian game hunters used to finish off a wounded animal by severing its uppermost cervical vertebrae. Typically, it is of a single-edged blade design with a stag-horn or bone grip, and was traditionally carried in a purpose-made pocket sewn into *lederhosen*. Knives of this design found their way into the trenches during the First World War where they were considered a status symbol by many regiments. *(See Lederhosen)*

*Jasta*—German, or "*Jagdstaffel*," was a squadron of German fighter planes during the First World War. *Jastas* are often associated with the garish paint schemes that were employed by the pilots to both personalize their aircraft and to develop squadron themes. *(See Flying Circus)*

*Junkers*—German, a term for the landed nobility of Prussia, which after 1871 had an important influence on the officer class of the Imperial German Army.

*Kaiser*—German, translates to English as, "emperor," and in this instance refers to *Kaiser Wilhelm II of Germany.*

*Kepi*—French, a circular cap made typically of wool of other soft materials that generally features either a visor or peak. The *kepi* was the standard issue headgear of the French Armed Forces at the outbreak of the First World War, but by 1915 had largely been replaced by the *Adrian* helmet for frontline duty due to the *kepi* offering little protections for the wearer. The *kepi* was then relegated to off duty, garrison, or parade use, yet was still worn by officers as a sign of rank. *(See Adrian)*

*Krampus*—German and Central-European, is a horned demon-like figure that is the antithesis of Saint Nicholas. Traditionally, the two are said to visit households together during the Christmas season, and whereas Saint Nicholas rewards children who have behaved throughout the year with gifts, *Krampus* punishes them for misbehaving, by some accounts even brutally.

*Lebel (Rifle)*—French, refers to the "*Lebel Model 1886 Rifle*," which was the standard infantry rifle used by the French armed forces during the First World War. Chambered in 8 x 50R mm (not to be confused with 8mm Mauser), it was a bolt-action, magazine-fed rifle featuring a tubular magazine capable of holding up to 10 rounds. Despite being obsoleted by the German military's '*Geweher 98*' of Mauser design the *Lebel Model 1886* continued to serve as the main battle rifle of the French armed forced throughout the conflict and beyond. *(See Coutrot, Gewehr 98)*

*Lederhosen*—German, literally translates to "leather breeches," are part of traditional German male garb consisting of rough leather shorts of various lengths with distinctive suspenders and a buttoned drop front. Originally designed for rough physical work, *lederhosen* gradually became part of essential German culture in the late 19th century, especially in regards to the Bavarian regions.

*Le Vengeur*—French, soldier's slang for the *'Couteau Poignard Mle 1916'* issue trench knife. The name is derived from the inscription some manufacturer's placed in the ricasso of the blade, 'Le Vengeur De 1870' (which translates to English as 'the avenger of 1870') a reference to the French loss in the Franco-Prussian War.

*Lorry*—a truck, or other large vehicle designed to carry heavy loads. *(See also Camion)*

*Madchen*—German, translates to English, "Girl."

*Marechaussee*—French, translates to English, "Constabulary, or gendarme."

*Mark*—Common German slang for "Papiermark." *(See Papiermark)*

*Mauser C96*—German, in reference to the *'Mauser Construktion 96'* model handgun that was first produced for civilian and military usage and later adopted by the Imperial German Army beginning in 1896. It was a large, heavy, and imposing firearm with a distinctive grip assembly (giving rise to the nickname 'The broom handle'), and at one point was considered the most powerful handgun in the world (when chambered in 7.63 x 25mm).

*Metz*—an ancient principal city in the northeast of France that was annexed to Germany as part of the terms of France's devastating loss in the War of 1870. At the time of the First World War Metz was still German territory, though was to be returned to France yet again after the conclusion of the conflict and Germany's subsequent loss. *(See War of 1870)*

*Minenwerfer*—German, literally translates to "mine launcher," was a class of short-range mortars originally designed to be used by pioneers to clear obstacles that larger artillery could not locate effectively just prior to the First World War. As the conflict wore on, however, *minenwerfers* were increasingly used as a means of bombarding opposing trench systems and were particularly effective due to their mobility and diminutive size. *(See Stokes Mortar)*

*Morning Hate*—a term used during the First World War generally in reference to either; the morning "stand-to," or "stand-to-arms," which was when front line soldiers were awoken daily an hour before dawn and ordered to man the *fire steps* and parapets of their trenches fully armed in preparation for an attack. Or, a ritualistic bombardment by artillery and/or machine gun fire which generally occurred at or before dawn. *(See Fire step)*

*Moselle*—is a large river that flows through Luxembourg, Germany, and France, and in regards to the latter is a principal feature of the old town quarter of the city of Metz.

*Nail, French Nail*—A generalized term referring to any locally fabricated stabbing weapon crudely manufactured from scrap iron or other broken pieces of military equipment. Typically, this term is applied to a loose French design manufactured from a clipped piece of barbed wire post.

*NCO*—A non-commissioned officer, or officer that has yet to obtain a commission, who generally holds the rank of Sergeant or lower.

*Neger*—German, translates to English, "negro."

*Nieuport*—French, was a French airplane manufacturer prior to the First World War, and who manufactured several models of fighter-type airplanes during the war for the French, British, and Russian flying services.

*Oberleutnant*—German, translates to English, "First Lieutenant."

*Oberst*—German, translates to English, "Colonel."

*Papiermark*—German, was the wartime currency of Imperial Germany following the outbreak of hostilities in 1914. *Papiermarks* continued to be the official currency of Germany after the war as well, and are often associated with the hyperinflation of the 1920s. *(See Mark)*

*Petard Raquette*—French, a crude form of hand grenade that was issued as a stopgap measure by the French military in direct response to the German

*'Stielhandgranate M1915'* during the First World War. Consisting mainly of a steel cylinder that was packed with high explosives and then wired to a wooden handle or board, it was detonated by a crude ignitor that operated by contact after being thrown (though the earliest models had to be lit by hand before throwing, often with a lit pipe or cigarette!). Only marginally effective at best, the *Petard Raquette* was superseded by several designs and largely disappeared from the battlefield by the end of the conflict. *(See Potato Masher, Stielhandgranate M1915)*

*Pickelhaube*—German, literally translates *"pickel-*point, *haube-*bonnet," was the official headgear adopted by the Prussian Army in the 1840s, and was still the standard issue headgear worn by the Imperial German Army from the onset of hostilities in the First World War until roughly 1916. It consisted generally of a body made of boiled leather, felt, tin, or in the cavalry's case metal, and was adorned with various insignia to indicate branch of service, origin of unit, etc. *(See Wappen)*

*Pinard*—French, a French term for wine, often used in reference to the wine ration given to French soldiers during the First World War.

*Pissoir*—French, is a structure used to house public urinals, which were prevalent in many major French cities from the mid-19th through the end of the 20th century.

*Place Saint-Louis*—is a public square in the old town quarter of Metz France, which began its life as an open-air market for grain and produce. By the time of the First World War, however, it had become a gathering place featuring cafes, restaurants, and pubs.

*Poilu*—French, an informal term for a French infantryman during the First World War, which literally translates to English, *'hairy one'* in reference to a generally unkempt appearance.

*Polackes*—German, a derogatory slur for someone of Polish descent.

*Polish POW's*—Despite Poland not officially existing during the First World War, her former citizens found themselves swept into the conflict and fighting for various belligerent nations just the same. During the course of the war, over three million Poles were organized into the Imperial Armed Forces of Austro-Hungary, Russia, and Germany, and in many incidences found themselves to be opposing forces on the same battlefield.

*Potato Masher*—Soldier's slang for the *'Stielhandgranate M1915'* issue German hand grenade, which was subsequently used in reference to all other stick-type grenades employed by Germany's armed forces through the Second World War.

*Prostituee*—French, translates to English, "prostitute."

*Reims*—a principal city in France that lays roughly 80 miles northeast of Paris and which sustained heavy damage during the First World War, particularly from German bombardment.

*Schnapps*—German, is a colloquial German term used in reference to any strong alcoholic drink, though is often used directly to refer to a drink made from fruits or herbs and consumed in small quantities in conjunction to a meal.

*Schneider (Artillery Piece)*—French, (in reference to Schneider—Creusot a major French steel and arms manufacturer), here refers to the *"Canon de 105mle 1913 Schneider,"* which was one of the heavier pieces of field artillery used by the French armed forces during the First World War. Larger and more powerful than the famed *75*, the *105 mm Schneider* was called upon in increasing numbers as the conflict settled down into static trench warfare. *(See 75, French 75)*

*Schweinshaxe*—German, is a dish in German cuisine consisting of a slow-roasted ham hock. This dish is particularly popular in the Bavarian regions of Germany.

*See the Elephant*—a colloquial term with origins dating from roughly the 16th century, it is often used in reference to seeing or experiencing something that made the individual seem worldly or experienced. The term *seeing the Elephant* later was adopted for military use to reference experiencing combat for the first time.

*Seine (River)*—is a major waterway that flows for over 400 miles through northern France, passing through the City of Paris before eventually emptying into the English Channel.

*Senegalese*—in reference to French *Senegalese Tirailleurs*, who were a corps of French infantry recruited from Senegal, French West-Africa, and other sub-Saharan regions of the French colonial empire. During the First World War, *Senegalese Tirailleurs* fought with distinction throughout the Western Front and other theatres and were known for their physical size and reckless bravery.

*Sergent*—French, translates to English, "Sergeant."

*"Si vous etes si interesse par les Allemands, puis-je suggerer que vous montiez reellement au front et que vous vous battiez? Je peux vous assurer que vous verrez beaucoup d'Allemands a ce moment-la, et je suis sur que certains d'entre eux seraient heureux de vous aider dans votre chasse au tresor"*—French, translates to English, "If you are so interested in the Germans, may I suggest that you actually go up to the front and do some fighting? I can assure you that you'll see plenty of Germans then, and I'm sure that some of them could assist you in your treasure hunt."

*Spatzle*—A type of egg-noodle pasta that is popular in the cuisines of Germany, Austria, and some Eastern European countries.

*Stahlhelm*—German, literally translates to "steel helmet," and is directly a reference to the steel helmets that began to replace the leather *Pickelhaube* helmets worn by the Imperial German Army beginning in 1916. Of the iconic coal-scuttle design, the models employed during the First World War are the M16, M17, and M18, respectively. *(See Pickelhaube)*

*Stirnpanzer*—German, was a heavy steel armor plate designed to be fitted to the front of a *Stahlhelm* helmet (M16, M17, or M18). It was intended to be worn by specialist soldiers only, such as snipers or trench sentries, due in part to its considerable weight which restricted the movement of the wearer. *(See Stahlhelm)*

*Stokes Mortar*—was a light mortar of British design that entered service in 1915. Capable of reaching targets up to 800 yards away and of firing upwards of 25 rounds per minute, the *Stokes Mortar* proved to be an extremely effective answer to the Imperial German Army's *Minenwerfer* and in fact continued to serve with various armed forced through the Second World War. *(See Minenwerfer)*

*Stollen*—German, vast underground bunkers that were typically dug 15 to nearly 50 feet below the surface, and were designed to safely house large quantities of infantrymen and war material during a counter-barrage or in preparation for a large-scale attack. *Stollen* were first employed by the Imperial German Army in preparation for the attack on Verdun, which began on the 21st of February, 1916.

*Stormtrooper*— 'Stormtroopers,' or 'Sturmtruppen' were specialist soldiers of the Imperial German Army during the First World War. Utilizing infiltration and shock tactics, *Stormtroopers* were primarily armed with hand grenades and specialized small arms and were focused on rapidly penetrating enemy territory, often with the element of surprise.

*Strudel*—A layered pastry that became popular in Austria during the 18th century before being adopted into German cuisine.

*Traverse*—(in reference to trench warfare, *traverse* has several definitions. Of the four most common definitions the one being referred to here is) an adaptation to trench construction in which crenellations or blind corners are configured into the trench line itself. By doing so, shrapnel and shock waves from explosions cannot travel past the obstacle the *traverse* creates, thereby creating the opportunity for shelter for defenders.

*Underberg*—German, a strong German digestif, or bitter liquor taken after a large meal to aid digestion.

*Very Lights*—or flares, which are fired out of a *Very pistol* (or flare-gun) to either send a distress signal or to illuminate an area briefly at night. During the First World War *Very Lights* were launched out of hand-held single-action pistols for various reasons: to send a general distress signal or to signal that one's trench was under attack, to help indicate artillery hits and misses, or to briefly illuminate a surrounding area at night to reveal suspicious activity to name a few.

*Von*—German, literally translates to "from, of," and is used in German and Austrian surnames typically to indicate nobility. *(See Junkers)*

*Wappen*—German, literally translates to "coat of arms," and in this instance refers to the brass or metal plate affixed to the front of a Pickelhaube helmet that indicated the origin of the unit that the wearer belonged to, e.g., opposing lions with a crested shield to represent Bavaria, an eagle, scepter, and globe to represent Prussia, etc. *(See Pickelhaube)*

*War of 1870*—Or the *Franco-Prussian War* was a conflict fought between the Second French Empire and the North German Confederation from 1870 to 1871, and was a military disaster for France that resulted in territory loss and the total collapse of its government.

*Wastage*—Military *wastage* is a term originally used by the British army to describe personnel loss not directly related to an attack. During the First World War *wastage* came to describe losses suffered by soldiers in their own trenches due to artillery attack, sniper fire, or other means. Due to the static nature of the conflict daily *wastage* numbers could be considerable, sometimes amounting to hundreds if not thousands of soldiers *per day* in particularly active sectors.

*Weissbier*—German, is an unfiltered wheat beer that is traditionally from the Bavarian region of Germany. The name *Weissbier* literally translates to "white beer," but the name *Weizenbier* (which translates to 'wheat beer') is sometimes used interchangeably.

*Willkommen Zuhause*—German, translates to English, "welcome home."

*Wristlet*—The term generally used for a military wrist watch during the First World War, which were a relatively new invention and were just coming into vogue versus the pocket watch.

*8mm Mauser (round)*—Is a smokeless rimless cartridge adopted by the German military to be the standard rifle ammunition of its armed forces in the late 19th Century. It was later used in the MG08 and MG08/15 machine guns as well which were the standard heavy machine guns of the German military during the First World War. This cartridge additionally served as the standard rifle/machine gun cartridge of the German armed forces through the end of the Second World War. (Note: actual cartridge dimensions are 7.92 x 57mm) *(See Gewehr 98, MG08/15)*

*75 (Artillery Piece)*—French, refers to the *"Canon de 75 Modele 1897,"* or *"French 75,"* which was the standard piece of French field artillery during the First World War. Widely considered to be the first modern artillery piece, it was originally designed to rapidly fire time-fused anti-personnel ammunition at targets advancing over open spaces. As such, as the conflict rapidly devolved into static trench warfare it was found that the flat trajectory and relatively small payload of the *75* was ill-suited to this new development. Despite these drawbacks, under the right circumstances it was still a formidable weapon, and it continued to serve throughout the entire conflict.

*220 Mortar (Artillery Piece)*—French, refers to the *"Mortier de 220 mm Tir Rapide modele 1915/1916 Schneider,"* which was an extremely heavy field mortar fielded by the French armed forces during the First World War. Of another *Schneider* design, it was capable of firing a projectile weighing over 200 lbs. up to 6 miles. *(See Schneider, Schneider-Creusot)*

*MG 08/15*—German, refers to a variant of the *'Machinengewehr 08'* or *'MG08'* which was the standard heavy machine gun of the Imperial German armed forces during the First World War. Chambered in 8mm Mauser, the *MG08* was a belt-fed crew-served weapon that was used in static positions as a defensive weapon, and as such regularly caused horrendous casualties to attacking forces throughout the conflict. The *MG08/15* variant was designed to be lighter, more mobile, and require a smaller crew than the *MG08*, and could even be operated by an individual infantryman when a 250-round drum attachment was utilized. In this new capacity, the *MG08/15* could be employed to provide substantial firepower to attacking infantrymen moving toward an objective and was particularly effective in this role. *(See 8mm Mauser)*

# Bibliography

Baldwin, Michael. (2018). *Feldzug 1918, Volume 5*. (First Edition). UK: Military Mode Publishing.

Bull, Stephen. (2016). *German Machine Guns of World War 1, MG 08 and MG 08/15*. (First Edition). UK: Osprey Publishing.

Hamilton-Paterson, James. (2015). *Marked For Death, The First War In the Air*. (First Edition). Great Britain. Head of Zeus Ltd.

Hanson, Neil. (2005). *Unknown Soldiers*. (First American Edition). US: Alfred A. Knopf.

Horne, Alistair. (1962, 1993). *The Price of Glory, Verdun 1916*. (Third Edition). England: Penguin Books.

Mirouze, Laurent. (1990). *World War I Infantry In Colour Photographs*. (Second Edition). Great Britain: Windrow & Green Ltd.

Remarque, Erich Maria. (1928, 1982). *All Quiet on the Western Front*. (Third Edition). US: Ballantine Books.

Sheffield, Gary (Editor). (2007). *War On The Western Front, In The Trenches Of World War I*. (First Edition). Great Britain: Osprey Publishing.

Traspaderne, Carlos. (2015). *The Tangier Archive, The Great War Photographs of Captain Givord*. (First Edition). England: Unicorn Publishing Group.

Printed in the USA
CPSIA information can be obtained
at www.ICGtesting.com
LVHW011608011023
759727LV00007B/121

9 781685 627843